LADIES OF THE
RACHMANINOFF
EYES

LADIES OF THE RACHMANINOFF EYES

HENRY VAN DYKE

WITH A FOREWORD BY ERIK WOOD

McNally Editions

New York

McNally Editions
134 Prince St.
New York, NY 10012

ISBN: 978-1-946022-88-2
E-book: 978-1-946022-89-9

Design by Jonathan Lippincott

1   3   5   7   9   10   8   6   4   2

For Carl Van Vechten

FOREWORD

If you were a young Black writer in America in the 1950s and early '60s, it was generally expected that you would write about struggle. It could be the struggle to put food on the table, or the struggle to walk down the street under the specter of racist violence, or the struggle to maintain your dignity in a world that wanted to degrade you; but one way or another (at least in the mind of well-meaning white readers), struggle was almost a mandatory theme. The same held true if you wrote as an out gay man. At that time, you were expected to write about inner struggle: self-hatred, defiance, darkness of heart. You might insist on the value of gay love, like Gore Vidal in *The City and the Pillar* or James Baldwin in *Giovanni's Room*; and if you were sufficiently defiant, you could depict the underworld of hustlers, like John Rechy in *City of Night*. Indeed, more and more Americans wanted to read about people on the so-called margins. What readers did *not* expect from a young Black novelist—certainly not one who was Black *and* gay—was that he should take his worth for granted, that he should shrug off the gay thing with nonchalance, or acknowledge racial hostility without a flash of rage, or that he'd choose the drawing room over the street, parody over satire, camp over tragedy, Rachmaninoff over the blues.

Then came *Ladies of the Rachmaninoff Eyes*, the first novel by my uncle Henry Van Dyke. Finished in 1961, rejected by a succession of publishers until finally published by Farrar, Straus and Giroux in 1965, *Ladies* is a comedy peeking out from behind the skimpiest of tragic masks. It tells of two elderly widows, Harriet Gibbs and Etta Klein, living together in the fictional Michigan town of Green Acorns. The ladies have bonded over their decades before the dawn of the '50s: "Harry" is Etta's longtime housekeeper. They share a love for Harriet's teenage nephew, Oliver; and an obsessive adoration for Etta's dead son, Sargeant, who five years earlier—spoiler alert/open secret—committed suicide after he moved to New York and fell in love with a Black man. (The Klein family is white and Jewish; Harriet and Oliver are Black.) Enter one Maurice LeFleur, a self-proclaimed warlock, who promises to summon Sargent's spirit from beyond the grave. Mayhem, as the saying goes, ensues.

As more than one critic noted, *Ladies* is an old-fashioned romp. A "light-decadent . . . confection," in the words of the *New York Times* reviewer. According to the *Kansas City Star*, "Henry Van Dyke now gives us cause to hope that the Burroughses, Rechys, and Mailers may at last be succeeded by writers as intent upon the elegant phrasing of their messages as upon the messages themselves." It's true. The fairy godfathers whispering in Henry's ear were not Rechy or Burroughs—or Baldwin, either—but Noël Coward and Ronald Firbank. And yet *Ladies* found appreciative readers in younger queer writers including

James Purdy and Iris Murdoch, on whom Henry harbored an enduring intellectual crush. The old tricks were being put to new uses.

Henry was born in 1928 in the small town of Allegan, in western Michigan. His mother's family, the Chandlers, had arrived there in the 1850s as free people, when there was already a thriving Black community. The first Van Dykes came a few years later, on the eve of the Civil War. Like many families, Black and white, Henry's forebearers had seen their fortunes rise with the tech boom of the early twentieth century, when corporations like Pfizer and Upjohn sprouted up around the railway hub of Kalamazoo. Henry's father, who went by Lewis, was a chemist; his mother, Bessie, an English teacher. In 1932, when Henry was four years old, they moved the family to Montgomery, Alabama. They had accepted professorships at the all-Black Alabama State Teachers College (later Alabama State University). In Montgomery they soon had two more children, daughters Barbara and Jackie.

The Van Dykes were prominent figures at Alabama State. Lewis would hold the position of Head of Arts and Sciences. The Reverend Martin Luther King, Jr., would officiate at Jackie's wedding. Rosa Parks was a family friend. The children were also conscious of being set apart as transplants. Although they attended the small, progressive Laboratory School on campus, Henry remembered having "only two playmates 'suitable' in my age range."[1]

---

1 This and other quotations are from Henry's unfinished memoirs, now in the archive of the Hopwood Awards program in the Special Collections Library of the University of Michigan.

In his isolation, he turned to books. Bessie's glass-fronted bookcase held more than the standard-issue Shakespeare, Milton, Keats, and Paul Laurence Dunbar. Henry was thrilled to discover *Lady Chatterley's Lover* sandwiched between more anodyne books.

The college campus was a relative safe space even though Alabama whites made clear the boundaries for Black folk. I spent a childhood summer there, with my grandparents, after the 1963 church bombing in Montgomery that killed four little Black girls. I recall, as clear as this morning, Bessie warning me not to step off the porch for fear that I would be mutilated. The Van Dyke children grew up in a kind of protective detention. As soon as Henry reached adolescence, Lewis began taking him on forays down country roads to view the dead bodies of lynched Black men. "Don't look away!" he would command. This was meant to preclude "any ideas of having sexual traffic with a white girl."

In fact, Henry was already—secretly and unhappily— attracted to other boys, and his perceived queerness was another source of anxiety at home. Lewis actively discouraged Henry's love of piano and forced him to go out for the football team. Hoping to "outgrow" his homosexuality, Henry would have several encounters with girls and women. The first, when he was thirteen, took place with two boys and a girl "from the wrong side of the tracks," and resulted in a pregnancy. The girl died from a back-alley abortion paid for by the three boys, who never spoke to each other again, and who kept the terrible secret. Henry's parents never found out.

Soon after, the Van Dykes returned to Michigan long enough for Lewis to complete his PhD. Compared to

Montgomery, Michigan was a kind of paradise to Henry: "I did not have to sit at the back of public buses; I did not have to drink from the tacky water fountain marked FOR COLORED ONLY . . . I did not see the repressed rage within my father from being called 'boy' by a traffic cop." Michigan also provided a refuge from his father's scrutiny and disapproval. When the rest of the family returned to Alabama, Henry stayed behind. He finished high school in Lansing and Kalamazoo, living with his Chandler relatives.

Family life for the Chandler clan unfolded in the two-story Italianate house in Allegan that Poppa Chandler had built himself. Teenaged Henry observed all the bickering and indulgence that one might expect among cousins. As an adult, he would grow to be the family storyteller, the one who could bring the most dramatic and expressive of his departed aunts and uncles back to life.

Henry graduated from high school in 1945 and enrolled at the University of Michigan in Ann Arbor. He planned to study music and become a concert pianist. When Lewis demanded that he take premed classes instead, Henry retaliated by dropping out and joining the army. He would come back to the university later, on the GI Bill, to study on his own terms. First, the army sent him to Germany, where he initially worked as a stenographer in the court martial system—a job he loathed—then he was recruited as second flautist to the (all-Black) 427th Marching Band, posted outside Heidelberg. In Heidelberg, he continued his musical education, taking private piano lessons under photos of his teacher, Franz Büchner, giving the Nazi salute. The rigidity of these lessons shook Henry in his ambition to become a professional pianist, although he continued to play all his life. He loved Scriabin, Poulenc, Granados, Albéniz, Liszt, Rachmaninoff always. Even at the end of his life, during his last weeks in hospice, he used paper keyboards to practice his fingering.

It was in the army that Henry started to write in earnest. He also started to explore his homosexuality, cruising Heidelberg's notorious "Philosopher's Walk" on the grounds of the old castle. There, he felt empowered. He was part of a victorious army among vanquished people, the reverse of his experience in white supremist Montgomery. His natural beauty, and the rarity of being Black in an ocean of whites, lent him an exotic allure. Henry returned to the University of Michigan in 1949, this time majoring in journalism. He wrote for the campus literary magazine and finished a novel, which won a college prize, although he never tried to have it published.

In Ann Arbor, Henry found a coterie of like-minded friends, most of them Black, most from the South, most from well-off families, all homosexuals. They relished commenting on classmates and movie stars and avidly musing about the sexual appetites of men who caught their eye. In his own words, Henry found Ann Arbor "offered everything emotionally necessary . . . great concert artists . . . lectures . . . sensibilities both sweet and belligerent . . . sex . . . books . . . lieder." He thrilled to the torch songs of Édith Piaf, Mabel Mercer, and Bobby Short, and to the high modernism of Gertrude Stein and Virgil Thomson, whose *Four Saints in Three Acts* became a talisman.

Henry's bohemian Ann Arbor also provided a cocoon for him at the height of the Civil Rights Movement.

He followed the 1955–56 Montgomery Bus Boycott at a distance, through what he and his sisters called Bessie's "Letters from the Front." For the thirteen months the boycott lasted, Lewis woke every morning at four o'clock to drive domestic workers to their jobs, returning just in time to shower and assume his administrative duties by eight o'clock. Bessie baked corn muffins for the riders. It is striking to me—it was striking to Henry, looking back—how completely he eschewed such current events in the fiction that he published in the campus magazine. "Perhaps I was running away," Henry later wrote. "This path, this vision, this lack of militancy carried straight on through to my first novel."

I suggest that, for its very lack of militancy, *Ladies* has to be one of the most unusual, most hopeful, and funniest novels to come out of the Civil Rights era. It is also unusually brave, for it is deeply autobiographical. The hero, Oliver, is clearly a Portrait of the Artist as a Gay Black Teen: undeclared in his sexuality, but queer to anyone with a clue. (The cluelessness of the people around him is a source of comedy throughout.) The ladies themselves are drawn directly from life, based on Henry's aunt Dayetta Chandler and on the real-life widow of a local executive. The setting offers an idyll—to use Henry's word, a "vision"—of inclusivity, where racial inequity and homophobia exist but are not crushing. In Green Acorns, Blacks and whites, Jews and gentiles, mistresses and servants, are able to annoy, love, despise, and lust after each other as individuals. Sexual identities are a matter of harmless confusion; the supposed "tragedy" of interracial or homosexual love is no more than a MacGuffin to animate a lighthearted, zany, not to say lunatic plot.[2] When Oliver attempts a half-hearted seduction of a white (female) neighbor, nobody says or thinks anything about lynching. In Green Acorns, a Black boy's love of Romantic music and French literature isn't cause for derision; it means a free ticket to Cornell from Mrs. Klein, who treats Oliver like a second son.

Henry wrote *Ladies* soon after he moved to New York City in 1958. Like many small-town writers before him, he found that New York gave him a clear-eyed view of the place he'd left behind. In New York he also found a new cosmopolitan tribe in piano bars, cocktail parties, and late-night cruising spots. He met many of his favorite musicians, including Bobby Short, who became a lifelong friend. He formed more complicated friendships with Virgil Thomson and Carl Van Vechten, another elderly pair whose relationship he would fictionalize (to hilarious effect) in the sequel to *Ladies*, *Blood of Strawberries* (1969), set in the Chelsea Hotel. When *Ladies* couldn't find a publisher, it was Van Vechten who advised Henry to rely even more on his ear for dialogue and his own glittering wit, to write the way he talked. Henry repaid that good advice by dedicating the book to him.

In New York, Henry could ferociously be his best gay self, and he was much recommended as a guide for visitors from out of town. So it was that he became friends with

---

2 As many a gay reader will note, this melodramatic element owes a good deal to the film *Suddenly, Last Summer* (1959), starring Katharine Hepburn and adapted for the screen by Truman Capote and Gore Vidal. This debt is cheerfully acknowledged early on in *Ladies* when Oliver bogarts his way into an unnamed Hepburn movie by presenting a stolen ticket.

the flamboyant and very social Edward Montagu-Scott, Baron of Beaulieu; his wife, Belinda; and many of their visiting friends, including the British writer Geraldine van Wiedman. Over a first lunch date at the Algonquin, van Wiedman asked to see the much-rejected manuscript of *Ladies*, then took it back with her to London, and to her editor at the publisher Hutchinson & Co. This editor, in turn, passed it to Roger Straus, the adventurous president of Farrar, Straus and Giroux, who happened to be in London, and who quickly wired Henry with an offer. Straus would go on to publish his next two books as well.

Ladies found its readers, but it's fair to say Henry was never a hit with the general reading public. Really, his public did not yet exist. The foibles of his characters are universal; anyone with a family can relate; but perhaps this was part of the problem. White readers were not used to finding Black characters treated with the same irreverence, neither more nor less, than whites. Nor, perhaps, were they ready to laugh with a Black gay man as the author and star of an effervescent, epigrammatic farce. Strange to say it now, but even many sophisticated people didn't know camp could be a Black thing. ("Camp taste is a kind of love, love for human nature. It relishes, rather than judges, the little triumphs and awkward intensities of 'character' . . . Camp is a tender feeling." Susan Sontag, 1964.) In this matter, at least, I think America knows better today.

Erik Wood
St. Louis, MO, 2023

LADIES OF THE RACHMANINOFF EYES

ONE

1

Aunt Harry died near the salt lick, on a Saturday daybreak in August, shortly after she and Mrs. Klein beat Maurice LeFleur almost to death with a stick in a patch of joe-pye weeds. Although it was too late, Mrs. Klein screamed: "Run, Oliver, her medicine! Run!"

For the second time that morning I ran past the hot-house, past the shed, through Mrs. Klein's kitchen and dark hallways, in slippers and pajamas. When I got back to the lawn, she said, "Oh, Oliver, look what Harriet's done. *Look* what she's done."

She had died. Mrs. Klein, in a housecoat, looked down at Aunt Harry's body with accusation, and a glossy cameo that dangled from her neck bumped Aunt Harry's black face. She was dead. There by the salt lick.

"Harriet? Harriet?" Her hand poked Aunt Harry, demanding she stop displaying some wicked joke, some spectacular disobedience. "Oh, Oliver, is she dead? Is she dead?"

The sun pushed up from the east scrubs; it was no longer daybreak. It was day, and Aunt Harry lay dead on the ground.

"Don't cry, Oliver, dearest, don't." She began pulling me to her, stepping on my slippers, pressing her wrinkled face into my neck. "Please, don't." A fragrance of walnuts came from her harsh white hair and cocks were crowing and sunlight was in my eyes.

I had no intention of crying. I would have liked to; it was appropriate. It was, of course, Mrs. Klein who was crying: Aunt Harry had been with Mrs. Klein forever—for thirty years—and it seemed, from the way she was consoling me, that the boundaries of my aunt's servitude had faded into a violent kinship. Nevertheless, Mrs. Klein said, as she looked over my shoulder to Aunt Harry's body, "She did it to spite me, Oliver, I know she did. Harriet? Harriet?"

Maybe. Certainly if it hadn't been for Maurice LeFleur she would be living. She'd be snapping at Bertram for not cleaning away cow dung; yelling at Della for not dusting in the crevices of the piano legs; she'd be watering down Mrs. Klein's breakfast rum; and she would be sniffing at my French grammar book, complaining about my "bone-lessness," and complaining that Mrs. Klein was ruining me by sending me to Cornell instead of a sensible school right there in Michigan, and that, as sure as anything, Mrs. Klein was trying to make a white boy out of me.

Still, it was too soon to cry: the sound of bickering, the sound of grumbling, was yet in my ears, and at the moment this sound was more real than the fact of her death at our feet; this was something—even for a minute—to hang on to. Had Mrs. Klein forgotten so soon the bickering and bantering, the fights? The sandwiches to be put in a picnic basket, and the sandwiches not to be put in a picnic basket?

The flavor of ice cream to be used on Sunday? And the rum? There always was a fight over the rum, particularly the hot rum drinks Aunt Harry made on rainy days. Mrs. Klein swore Aunt Harry's creation was a watered-down cough syrup and juice of lemon.

"Heavens, Harriet," she often said when she was given the drink, "I need to send you to bartender's school. Did you put any rum in it?"

We watched Mrs. Klein bend her heavy nose to the brew the second time; only the rain on the bay windows made a sound. Aunt Harry's face was alert, waiting, under piles of white fiberglass hair. "Well?"

"Slop, Harriet. Absolute slop. Why, I can't taste a thing but syrup."

Aunt Harry turned away. "That's because you're an alcoholic, that's why. Rum for breakfast. Rum puddings. Rum salads. How do you expect to taste anything when rum's the natural state of your taste anyway?"

Mrs. Klein looked at me and tightened her lids in a half wink so all the wrinkles would stand out. She must have guessed how much all those labyrinthian paths leading to her blue eyes fascinated me. "Your aunt's exaggerating again, dear. She does so like to exaggerate. Don't you like to exaggerate, Harriet? Harriet? Oh, Harriet, don't be tedious—*you* started it."

Aunt Harry placed Dresden china on the table in front of us. "I just said you're an alcoholic. I stated a fact. That's all I ever do—state facts."

A rose tinge came to Mrs. Klein's chalk in her cheeks. "But, really, now, I don't drink that much. You think I drink that much, Oliver?"

"I—"

"If you was to die tomorrow, Etta Klein, they'd be afraid to cremate you with all that alcohol you've got in you. You'd start a conflagrating fire."

"Foot," Mrs. Klein said, tapping the black satin around her brooch. "Isn't she a comedian, Oliver, conflagrating, ha! I don't think she's funny at all." Her laugh, with mahogany teeth, was the sound of soft rifle shots, but quickly she stopped it and turned towards Aunt Harry and the silverware. "Anyway, I may not get cremated, I may have Jerome bury me."

"You'll get cremated."

"Not if I don't want to."

"All Jews get cremated, don't they?"

Mrs. Klein drew out a grand handkerchief of Brussels lace. "Dearest Harriet, you're so ignorant about Judaism. That's one area I think you ought to just stay clear out of."

"Well, I'm only going by what I've heard and what I've seen. You cremated Sargeant didn't you? You had your own son cremated. Now just try to tell me that that's exaggerating."

Quietly Mrs. Klein looked dead into Aunt Harry's dark face, dabbing all the while her Brussels lace to her goitered neck. "Sargeant, Mrs. Gibbs, *asked* to be cremated. He *chose* to be cremated. Sargeant . . . Sargeant . . ."

I never knew what to do about ladies crying, and at Green Acorns both of them cried usually at the same time or in close sequence. Once, earlier in June, when then they thought Della was made pregnant by a farm equipment salesman from Chicago (she wasn't; Della lied to soften them up for a raise in salary), they both began to cry—Mrs. Klein in barking, suffering noises, and Aunt Harry in a whinny. I had said, "Stop, Mrs. Klein, it's all right," and then I ran over to console Aunt Harry with "Now, now, Auntie, it's all right," and then back again to Mrs. Klein. It was a relay race of sorts.

But worse was the aftermath: Mrs. Klein, who apparently needed to pay penitence for an excess of sentiment, chose me to help her expiate her venial weakness: we would dig weeds in the hot sun, or wash PG, the cat, or sometimes it took a cerebral form and I would read to her Wordsworth poems. With Aunt Harry the aftermath of a crying spell was less physical but no less painful. Admonitions and sneers came from her pony face, a face chockfull of wrath. "I'm ashamed of you. Sucking up to that white woman just as if she was your dear, dead Mama. Nibbling at her petticoats, Oliver Eugene, that's what I call it." And if I tried to point out that I was *consoling* (during that relay race) *both of them*, she'd say: "Yeah? but you was with her the most. You'd think blood relations didn't mean anything whatsoever the way you act. You ought to pay more attention to family ties, Oliver Eugene. There's nobody left of all of us but you and me. You and me, Oliver. We're the last of the whole family tree, and what do you do? You suck up to old Mrs. Klein like *she* was your relative instead of me. Just because she's sending you to that fancy college to study and you can say a few fancy French words, you think I don't count for anything, don't you?" I learned some time ago that I could place my hands on her fiberglass hair and bury my face in her starchy collar—she was as tall as God; I'm six one—and murmur (which I admit is a dirty trick): "Don't fuss at me, Auntie, please don't fuss at me." Of course, Aunt Harry wanted, right then and there, to burn her tongue out. "Poor lonely boy. In a big old house with two old ladies. Harriet Gibbs, you must pray to God," etc.

Oh, I knew their tears would stop; they'd begin with a noisy jolt, just like the shower in the west room and like the shower, their tears would stop without warning. But meanwhile I had to placate such opposite souls with the same words, the same frightened nonsense. And they did frighten me—those ladies with tears coming out of their ancient eyes, wetting the millions of wrinkles around their eyes, as though to irrigate the cracked parchment around their eyes, those eyes so like old pictures of Rachmaninoff's eyes. Moreover, their indelicacy frightened me. What was I to do? Walk out of the room? Run to the black grove of trees where the acorns fell? And now this crying, an indecent duet, was instigated by Aunt Harry's quip about Sargeant, Mrs. Klein's bachelor son, who slashed his wrists in New York City, in a Sutton Place bathtub, five New Year's Eves ago. (Why? Aunt Harry claims she knows why, but she doesn't.)

I particularly didn't like them to cry about Sargeant, for it placed me in an awkward position. It wasn't that I was taking Sargeant's place exactly—I was more or less the "project" used to fill in Mrs. Klein's time, though on this matter Aunt Harry had two opinions: she would say to the townspeople of Allegan, "With all of Mrs. Klein's millions from the stoves they make in Kalamazoo she can well afford to educate a poor unfortunate." (In public I was a poor unfortunate, who was going to attend school out East; back at the edge of town, at Green Acorns, I was a "boneless" specimen who should have been going to a decent school right there in Michigan.)

Jerome, Mrs. Klein's other son, thought it noble of his mother to educate me, buy me Chesterfield coats, English tweeds, first editions of dull classics. He never questioned what she did with her money; he had his own: he now controlled Klein Stove Manufacturers, and his twin boys were well taken care of at Harvard. To him I was his mother's toy. He meant, but never said, *her toy to keep her mind off Sargeant.*

It would be generous to think that Mrs. Klein took to rum right after Sargeant's suicide, but—according to Aunt Harry—Mrs. Klein leaned towards rum ever since Aunt Harry took up service with the Kleins some thirty-odd years ago. "You were drinking rum when Al Smith was running for President, Etta Klein," Aunt Harry said one Sunday over a quince on muffin.

Mrs. Klein was smoking an English Oval and reading her horoscope magazine. "At least one thing," she said, not looking up, "I was true to my Ezra when he was alive, Mrs. Gibbs. That's more than you can say for yourself, I'll wager. Oh, you think I didn't hear the gossip those days when we lived in Kalamazoo. Ha! Remember that little cook we had with the stutter? What was her name? Judith? Judith, yes. Judith said once that you were walking down Burdick once—"

"It's a lie, you know it's a lie, I never even looked at another man 'til the day Gideon Gibbs killed hisself by working his fool head off. For what? For the Klein family who didn't 'preciate him no how. Doubling as chauffeur, yardman, every thingamajig. Lord, it might've been the

11

Depression days, but you wasn't all *that* depressed. Slave labor. I thought many times of putting the NAACP on the whole lot of you."

Mrs. Klein frowned at her cigarette; it wasn't drawing; it was unlit. "Oh, hush, Harriet, you don't even know what the NAACP is."

(I was occupied with smoked oysters and quince with a glutton's concentration, but I was a bit uncomfortable; I never knew how much of the fight between the two ladies was real, how much was diabolical jest, how much was hate, how much was love. These games were always played in the same deadpan key.)

"Listen, Oliver," Aunt Harry said, rolling English muffin crumbs from her gums, "just to show you how cheap the Kleins were in those days—listen. Your great-uncle Gideon Gibbs worked like a slave. He drove that silly old limousine of theirs like a prince. He loved that car. But you think they 'preciated that? Gideon, believe me, had to take his *own* money to polish the thing. Why, they wouldn't even buy him a chauffeur's uniform. They—"

"Harriet! Now, you needn't go into—"

"They wouldn't even buy him a chauffeur's uniform—until one day! Oh, Lord, I think I'll never forget that day! One day Gideon drove Etta downtown to pick up some visiting business gentlemen of Mr. Klein's. This is hysterical. One day—"

"Now, Harriet, I don't think it's necessary that Oliver know this. It was a long time ago, for heaven's sake."

Aunt Harry's eyes were cat glints, gleaming like PG's do on her evil days. "First of all, your great-uncle Gideon was very light-skinned. You seen pictures of him on my bureau. In point of fact, he looked far more white than Jerome does—and his hair wasn't even a third as kinky as Jerome's is. In point of fact, he could've passed for white any day. In point of fact, he *did* once in Birmingham, Alabama. He ate in a white restaurant and went to a white hotel, and slept in a white bed, and went to a white picture show. He had the time of his life being waited on by white folks. That trip was *some*thing, the way he told it. In point of fact, he took it just to *prove* he could get away with it. Some fellows in Chicago where he grew up—"

"Mississippi, I'll wager," Mrs. Klein said.

"—where he grew up made a bet with him. If Gideon didn't get caught and get lynched and got back to Chicago all in one piece, these fellows would treat him to dinners and drinks for a whole month. Gideon did it, Oliver, and it did take guts, because Gideon did look *sort* of colored if you looked real careful and there was a chance he'd get caught but—"

"Really, Harriet, can't you talk without jiggling the coffee all over the place? If this sloppiness continues, I'll be forced to take my breakfast alone, without jabbering servants around—That doesn't mean you, Oliver, dear."

"*Anyway*, Oliver, Gideon was white as a colored man could get without being actually white. So, these cheap Kleins in nineteen thirty-four asked Gideon to buy his *own* chauffeur's uniform. Course Gideon wouldn't. He was too principled, Gideon was. And he was neat. I pressed his best suit—and that cost us, too, I'll have you know—and he wore it with a white shirt and a tie. Then this day comes. Etta went to downtown Kalamazoo—and it seemed like a downtown ought to be, not all spread out like it is now—and picked up her husband's—God rest Ezra Klein—business gentlemen. They just beamed and beamed, those business gentlemen did, and Etta was as polite as pie when she got out on the sidewalk to meet them. But when they got in the car—you know what? You know what one of them said? One of them said, 'You sure do keep a fine-looking car, E.J.' He said this to Gideon and I sure wish I'd been there to see his friends hush him up. All of them, Gideon told me, practically had hemorrhages right there in the car seat."

"Harriet!"

"Well? Is it true or isn't it true? Come on, now, tell Oliver if it's true or not."

"Yes, it's true, but it was an understandable mis—"

"So, sweetie, can you guess what old E. J. Klein and Etta did the very next day? They went right in their so-called depressed pockets and bought your great-uncle Gideon a uniform! The bluest, brassiest, most chauffeurish uniform this side of the Alleghenies. Isn't that right, Etta?"

"Oh, for God's sake, Harriet, yes, that's right."

I was amused by that sort of gossip, those kinds of tidbits, and I would have listened all day, but something always broke into their ballades. Today it was the memory of Sargeant's Sutton Place suicide.

2

Handkerchiefs were out for the drying of eyes when Della came into the room, her maid's cap thumb-printed, her dress too tight. She took one look, and said, "Oh, Jesus Christ, not again," and turned sharply on her drumstick legs.

"Della! Della!" Aunt Harry shouted, her voice damp and foggy. "You come right back here and apologize for that remark!"

Della was twenty-eight and liked men very much. She said she was from Trinidad; Aunt Harry said Georgia. (She tried to crawl into bed with me one Thursday night and I thought it was PG and screamed. She said she'd never speak to me again.) "I apologize, I apologize, will you be having ginger cookies, Mrs. Gibbs?"

Mrs. Klein said, like la dame aux caméllias (chubby-style), "Must we?"

"Ginger cookies, Della. You can go. Go on, girl. Yes, we must, you know very well we must. You know that and then ask me 'must we.'"

"Jerome, Jerome. How do you know he likes those dreadful little baked goods? He's never had any chance to find out differently and naturally he's going to pretend to adore them. You and Jerome. Just because he always calls you 'Mrs. Gibbs' you think you must put him next to God."

Possessiveness sneaked into Aunt Harry's long face. She apparently felt it showing, for she began to do busywork with the pleats in her green tea dress. "Jerome," she said, "is a good man and I'm very proud he is."

"Regardless, I hate the very thought of those ghastly ginger things," Mrs. Klein said. "So—so homey."

"Everything is homey at Green Acorns."

"Thanks to you. Oliver, pet, run in the pantry and get another bottle of rum. The green label. I think I'll have just a bit with tea when Jerome comes. Here, and take these magazines and hide them somewhere. I don't want him to raise any kind of stupid fuss."

I deposited *Your Stars*, *Gemini & Others*, and *Paths of Direction* in the bread hamper, and picked out the emptiest of the nine opened bottles of rum. (Aunt Harry had an unswerving belief that the rum would disappear sooner if all the bottles were in use; at least she could *see* some progress towards the depletion of the supply, she claimed. It had occurred to me more than once that perhaps Aunt Harry drank secretly, and theft from many bottles in an unfinished state was less easily detected than was theft from one.) Just as I began to close the pantry door I noticed a clipping on the floor—I must have dropped it from one of Mrs. Klein's magazines. In cloudy type, on rough paper, it said:

MAURICE LEFLEUR

Warlock

&

Psychic Reader
Spiritualistic Consultant

REASONABLE	CHICAGO
RATES	BOX 122

The advertisement started a giggle within me, but it curdled and clogged in my throat: Would either of the two ladies take it seriously? Aunt Harry believed in omens, and of course Mrs. Klein read horoscope magazines with greed. But a *warlock*? In the want ads?

The pantry was damp, and smelled of rum, and it was dark there.

"I don't care *how* nonreligious she is," Mrs. Klein was shouting, waving her pink fists over the fragile china, "she is still a—"

The rainfall had muffled the sound of my steps as I came in from the pantry. I almost heard—heard *the* words from her lips. For some reason neither of the ladies would discuss the matter of Jerome's wife in front of me. I could only guess what crisis had once gripped them. The main trouble apparently, and the crux of the irritation, was that Jerome's wife—according to Aunt Harry's news clippings—was née Walker. *Captain Klein and his young bride, Patricia Jo Klein (née Walker) will spend two weeks at the Lake Michigan resort, Tri-Lodge, prior to Captain Klein's departure for overseas*, and so forth. (Aunt Harry insinuates that she, like the Nurse in *Romeo and Juliet*, had a great deal to do with the controversial union, but she didn't.)

It took Mrs. Klein several minutes and a sip of rum before she could readjust to the approaching ritual of

Jerome for tea. Her satin frock seemed cold and its black sheen caught in her white hair for moments at a time. A dull brooch on her flat bosom looked at me, and sometimes her blue eyes looked at me, too. But she was thinking of—of what? Sargeant? Jerome? Huge baby-faced Jerome with his reddish hair and his dirty jokes. Jerome and his laughing. I wondered what Sargeant was like, what magic he held, even in death, to wedge such distance between his mother and the living son. Certainly Patricia Jo Klein (née Walker) hadn't smashed a very deep love. It was at times like this, when she was thinking of Jerome or Sargeant, when her eyes looked at me and didn't see, that I wanted to dodge those eyes; those little pale eyes were grotesque when there was no life in them.

I cleared my throat and smiled, but she would not refocus her gaze. Aunt Harry was foolishly polishing the tea server, as though she hadn't just polished it last Saturday with the same vigor.

"Are you sad?" I asked. "Does the rain make you sad? You look sad."

She turned to the window, touching the brooch at her bosom with the forefingers of each hand. "Why, why, no, Oliver, I was just thinking how beautiful I was once."

Why I thought this a cue to laugh I don't know, but I did, falsely, with no cooperation from anyone.

Mrs. Klein woke up. "I was!"

"She sure was, Oliver." Aunt Harry's eyes were full of dark fires. "She was a tiny thing. A real beauty."

I hadn't really wanted to laugh. "Were you—were you living in Kalamazoo then? When you were pretty, I mean?"

"There. Oh yes, there. And Long Island for many years. I think that's when Sargeant got New York in his blood. You know he loved the elevated train more than any single— Oh, yes! Harriet, do you remember that awful row I had with Ezra?"

"Which one, dear?" Aunt Harry was sitting beside Mrs. Klein, practically holding her hand. It was too dizzying, this sudden pro-Mrs. Klein spirit; I simply could not decipher their game: at this moment these ladies were in love.

"*You* remember." Mrs. Klein laughed, barked, and moisture came to her eyes. "The time I rode in the car with no clothes on to bitch him."

They hugged! They snickered! Mrs. Klein's black satin arms were around Aunt Harry, and Aunt Harry's green cotton arms were around Mrs. Klein. They giggled and I could hear Della's tea water hissing through the rain.

"You tell him," Mrs. Klein said.

"No, no, I couldn't."

"You re*mem*ber."

Aunt Harry shook her fiberglass head and wiped tears from her eyes. "Oliver wouldn't understand anyway. It's not funny to tell. You tell him."

"Well, get together on it and tell. *You* were *nude* in a *car*, Mrs. Klein?"

She blew her nose and lit an English Oval. "It was in the thirties. You weren't even born. Mr. Klein and I had an awful row over some—some nonsense. You know, Harriet, I can't really remember—really clearly—what the whole thing was about. Anyway, I was shopping late in Manhattan. There was a summer rain, too, like today. All the way from Fifty-Ninth Street on Fifth Avenue . . . to the public library . . . I made Harriet's husband put his cap over the mirror . . . Oh, Harriet, I can't, I simply can't."

Aunt Harry dug her hard brown fingers into Mrs. Klein's chubby pink wrists and shook her face with a strange mirth, as though the Holy Ghost had touched her.

"I was young," Mrs. Klein whispered. "And silly. And so full of living."

"And you were beautiful."

"Yes, I suppose. I was beautiful, wasn't I?"

It stopped raining. Della was whistling *How long, how long, have that evenin' train been gone*, and my ladies of the Rachmaninoff eyes were reminiscing, in their widowhood, beyond my reach. From the window I looked at the silence of the afternoon, out where bluejays flew through an acre of trees hunting for a lunch; odors from the earth came through the windowpane, and then I walked over to the ladies and asked quietly, "Who is Maurice LeFleur?"

Had I said Jesus Christ was an Eskimo, or that Paris is a trashy town, there wouldn't have been as much perturbation. They both stood, digging their fingers into black satin and green cotton. Aunt Harry's stiff white collar was askew and Mrs. Klein's trembling hand knocked a fragile cup to the floor.

Mrs. Klein whispered: "Is he here?"

Aunt Harry ran to the window. "No, no. Only the bluejays and Bertram in the yard. You, you impudent little snippet. What do you mean, scaring years off our lives like that? How did you find out about Maurice LeFleur? What do you know about Maurice LeFleur?"

"The clipping, Auntie. Here. It fell out of *Gemini & Others*. I couldn't help but read—" One hand snatched the advertisement and her other hand fell across my mouth. I think I objected to the snatching hand the most.

"I don't give a damn if you want to converse with warlocks or anything else. I just picked the sick thing off the floor."

"Young man! You can stop this very minute! There never has been and never will be any swearing in this house, and I mean that. Understand?"

Pale as porcelain, Mrs. Klein sat down in her seat just as a horn blew, a long way off, at the foot of the drive. "Jerome. It must be Jerome."

"It is!" Aunt Harry said, pressing her nose to the pane. (She couldn't see that far, even with her glasses on.) "Della! The tea, Della. And Oliver, look happy. I don't want any sad faces with tea, now. Spruce up."

Jerome was hardly worth sprucing up for. I was sick of his "Oliver, old bean" and his "That's the way the ball bounces" and his "That's the way the cookie crumbles," and his dirty jokes he brought me each week, and like clothes for the needy, they were worn, shabby, and used. Last week it had been: "Say, old bean, you hear this one? Some people dip snuff, many smoke, but Fu Manchu. Ha-ha! Ha-ha!"

Jesus, what would it be this week? Irish cops, movie stars, traveling salesmen? Would ever he dare a Rastus cycle?

"Oliver, sweet," Mrs. Klein said, "run down and meet him, will you? Poor Bertram'll shout his lungs out—as if we couldn't hear Jerome's car a mile off."

He was overweight again, his lips were faintly stained from cigar ends, and his red hair was crisp from the damp air. "The old ladies been up to any rough stuff this week, old bean?" His laugh was sandpaper to the ear.

"Mrs. Klein kicked PG last Tuesday and Aunt Harry used the Lord's name in vain when she broke a sherbet glass." (Both were lies, but what else could I do, face to face with my Bringer of Glad Tidings of Great Joy?) "How is Mrs. Klein, Jerome?" I disliked thin and shrill Patricia Jo Klein née Walker, but it was always good public relations to inquire.

"Fine, fine. Anxious to get to Bermuda but I can't for a while yet. Say, kid, I heard a new one in town the other day, it's about these two queer spiders. You heard about the two homosexual spiders?"

"No."

"They played with each other's flies. Ha-ha! Ha-ha!"

"That's a dandy." The tops of my cheeks felt tawdry.

"Get it? They were playing with—"

"Yeah, yeah, I get it. It's a killer, all right, Jerome. You picked it up at KSM?"

His thick hand was still beating my shoulder. "Somebody in the plant started it. You know how those things spread . . . playing with each other's flies . . . Tea ready?"

Two satin arms, as though she were beginning a Martha Graham dance, went up in the air to embrace Jerome as he came into the room. Aunt Harry waited her turn for an embrace and the ritual began.

"How are the twins, dear boy?"

"Got word from the Cod not too long ago. Loving the sun. Eating it up. Patricia Jo is upset about them running with the wrong crowd, but you know Patricia Jo. Humidity. Nerves. Bermuda'll do her good."

Aunt Harry watched Jerome wash down two ginger cookies. "When do you leave for Bermuda, Jerome?"

"About ten days. Maybe sooner. There's a chance sooner. Slim chance."

"Good! See, Etta? Maurice LeFleur could—"

The table jiggled and Mrs. Klein was turning pink. "More tea, Jerome? Here, have some more tea. Come, come, Oliver, you've hardly touched yours."

Through a ginger cookie Jerome said, "Maurice, Mrs. Gibbs? Who's Maurice?"

"Did I say Maurice? Imagine that. Whatever made me say 'Maurice'?"

Jerome turned to me, and I looked down into the amber tea.

"Have a bit of rum, Jerome. It's so good in the tea. A bit? A little bit?"

Jerome jerked his neck around to free his flesh from his tight collar. "Come on, what's this Maurice business? Something's up. I can feel it. Come on, Mrs. Gibbs, tell old Jerry boy."

Aunt Harry's hand flew out of her lap to pat his knee. "Ah, Jerome, you know how an old woman babbles. I must have meant something else. You know me."

Like a game of tennis, Jerome's tender red hand reciprocated by patting Aunt Harry's green pleats. "Indeed I do," he said, grinning at me, fearing his delicious reply would go unappreciated. "Now, suppose, now—suppose I don't go to Bermuda, Mother. Suppose I stay right in Kalamazoo.

Suppose instead I come to Allegan for the weekends—for a few good old family get-togethers."

Indulgent, trembling lips parted and showed Mrs. Klein's mahogany teeth. "You know very well you can't deny Bermuda to Patricia Jo. It wouldn't be fair. And besides, those bedrooms need repapering and there'd be a cooking problem what with just Della, and you'd get bored with the place in two hours, now wouldn't you?"

Jerome was silent. It made both of the ladies fidget, and finally, as though she were compelled to confess under the pressure of silence, Mrs. Klein said softly, with flippant eyebrows, "Actually we might have a visitor for a couple of days."

"Oh?" Jerome turned to Aunt Harry and said again, with the same intensity, "Oh?"

"Yes, a visitor," Aunt Harry replied, her hands trying to explicate, form an image.

Jerome contemplated a cigar and then rolled it back and forth on the tea table. "A friend?"

"Yes, yes, a friend." This was going to be the end of it as far as Mrs. Klein was concerned: she and Aunt Harry had sailed past the rough waters.

"Who?" Their chuckling and casual guest was not being chuckling and casual. Aunt Harry would have probably retreated into some domestic activity would such flight not smack of desertion in the face of the enemy. Mrs. Klein, who was agile in noisy battle but terrified of its silences, began making death-rattling sounds in her throat. With rum-tea in hand, she said, "Mr. LeFleur. Mr. Maurice LeFleur."

"Yes, Mr. Maurice LeFleur," Aunt Harry echoed.

"A friend," said Mrs. Klein.

"For a couple of days," said Aunt Harry.

"About next week," said Mrs. Klein.

"Yes, next week," said Aunt Harry.

"Who is he?" said Jerome.

"A specialist," Aunt Harry said.

"A warlock," I said.

"A *who*?" Jerome asked, finally lighting his damned cigar.

Both Aunt Harry and Mrs. Klein looked at me hopefully; would I be their ally? Did I know what a warlock was? I strongly suspected they did not. "A warlock, Jerome, is—oh, it's sort of a charlatan. He reads tea and stuff. Actually, it's all harmless nonsense, but actually he's suppose to be sort of a male witch who—"

"Oliver!" Aunt Harry stood up. "Now, stop making jokes!" The lilt at the end of her demand betrayed her; her old eyes said: *Is that really so?*

"He is, Auntie. What do you think a warlock is?"

Mrs. Klein pulled her nose from her cup and spoke with authority. "Maurice LeFleur is a gentleman."

"You know him, Mother?"

"Not exactly. No, I wouldn't say exactly that I know him, no."

"At all? A little bit, Mother?" The deadly question came: "Have either of you ever *seen* this Mr. Le-whichamacallit?"

The world in the living room was falling apart, but Della was still whistling in the back of the house, *How long, how long, have that evenin' train been gone.*

"Have you?"

"No."

"No."

"Well," Jerome said, unsure of what to do with his victory. "So, that's the way the ball bounces. What'd you say a warlock was, Oliver? Get me a dictionary. God Almighty, this is why I'll have a coronary thrombosis. Christ, what is this? Inviting a stranger to Green Acorns you don't even know. Some sick bastard to boot. What is this? You both going batty at the same time?"

Jerome was pacing the floor, spitting out stinky blue clouds of smoke as I left for the study to fetch a dictionary. "Oliver," Mrs. Klein called after me, "there's . . . bring the dictionary, dear."

With reading glasses and PG on her lap, Mrs. Klein took the opened big unabridged dictionary. "Let's see. Warlock." She pitched her voice for an oratory. "'Warlock, a word seemingly used in northern English or Scottish for a wizard, sorcerer or magician; in O. Eng. *woerloga*, literally "a liar against the truth," from *wær*, truth, cognate with Lat. *verum*, and *loga*, liar, from *leogan*, to lie. It was used for a traitor, deceiver, breaker of a truce.'"

After a silence—all of us standing except Mrs. Klein— Aunt Harry said, "Goodness, all of that?"

Jerome examined the words Mrs. Klein could not, or would not, pronounce, and started his pacing again. "Where did you hear of this man?"

The ladies handed over the clipping and waited for him to read it, but Jerome shook his head right away. "Not on your life. Don't bring that crook in this house, old dears. This shyster'll strip the place clean. Clean, do you understand?"

Ordinarily this would have ended it, for the ladies respected Jerome's management ability, his business acumen, but their disappointment was deep, bitter. "All right, all right," he said roughly, "what in the dickens you want him for anyway? To read some silly tea cups? Cards? This would be a mighty expensive amusement, don't you think? Tell me if you want it and I'll hire a gypsy tea-reader to come out to the place if you want. But Jesus H. Christ, not this goddamn Chicago crook!"

Tears came to Mrs. Klein's eyes. "You don't know that, Jerome. You don't know that."

"I don't know it? What proof do you *need*, Mother? Listen, Mother, these kind of crooks live off this kind of foolishness. I know. I know. Mrs. Gibbs, *do* something. Show her how foolhardy it is."

Aunt Harry shook her head. "We already wrote to him to come."

"You what?"

"We already wrote to him to come. Your mother and me fixed up a letter two days ago. You needn't worry. I can watch him. Oliver'll help, too. I think anyway he's a gentleman, just like your mother says."

"You *think.* Jesus! Mary! and Joseph! Have you both gone batty? What you need him for anyway? What you need him out here for?"

Della came in with another batch of warm ginger cookies, but before she could put them down, Jerome waved his cigared hand. "Hell, no, get out."

"Jerome!" Mrs. Klein spoke sharply, but happily, almost as though she welcomed the role of mother scolding son. "That's no way to talk to Della."

Della's buttocks were rolling back to the kitchen, and she turned briefly, not in anger, but with—as though she had a kind of salacious itch, and she looked boldly at Jerome.

"Why did you pick him?" I said.

The ladies conferred with one another, without speaking. Aunt Harry finally said, looking down at her green pleats, "Because the name was so pretty. Maurice LeFleur. Somebody with a name like Maurice LeFleur can't be as bad as you say, now can they, Jerome?"

His cigar ashes fell in the ginger cookies. "Like hell he can't." Jerome was leaning over the table, pounding his fist, rattling china. "Do I have to hire a nurse to come out here and take care of you? Both of you? But—but, look at it, this ad. It's a fake. Can't you see it's a fake?"

"Why, dear?" Aunt Harry asked him so simply that it made Jerome swallow five or six times in a row; he knew very well that he was not pouring (successfully, at any rate) oil on troubled waters.

"And I thought," Mrs. Klein added in a distant, hurt voice, "we'd try to say hello to Sargeant. These things are done, Jerome, even if some say they aren't. If you just try a little they are done. My horoscope says—"

With both of his heavy tender hands Jerome banged on the table, his cigar skidding across the rug. "No, no, no, no! How many times—how many—" His head hung between his fleshy shoulders; his hand gripped a pattern of flowers on the lace of the tablecloth. Neither of the ladies seemed to notice a spilled cup of tea, a crackdown the face of the sugar bowl. I thought Jerome would cry. I never really knew how he felt about Sargeant. I never knew if he loved him or envied him. I never heard him mention Sargeant. "I've *told* you, Mother, I've told you a million times I've told you. Where's that ad?" He found it, wet with tea, and headed towards the phone in the study. "I'll send a wire. You can't see this goddamn crook. You can't see him, and that's all there is to it."

The sound of shouting evaporated.

"We can't see him, Harriet."

"We can't see him, Etta."

It was so sinister, the way they said it, with voices of resignation, but at the same time there were (or did I just imagine it?) gritty glints in their eyes; and on their laps of green cotton and black satin their fingers made patterns in hysteria.

PG danced a kind of four-step around Jerome's legs as he phoned his secretary in Kalamazoo to cancel an invitation to a warlock. Aunt Harry and Mrs. Klein heard it all, for the study door was ajar, but they sat tall in their chairs, heads half bowed, in prayer attitudes, silent. Della was humming her blues . . . *long, have that evenin' train been gone* . . .

3

"Aunt Harry said you could clear away the tea things, Della." These were my first words to her since that night she tried to crawl in my bed.

"I can, can I?" Della's large hazel eyes dominated her beige face; her bosom—obscene, really—dominated the rest of her. "Is Jerry still in there with 'em?"

"You mean *Mister* Klein?"

"Mr. Klein my ass. Now, how you sound?" She lit a cigarette and sank her gelatinous flesh into the edge of the old-fashioned kitchen sink. "You give me the gut ache with all your prissy airs. Lord, how I'd like to see your feathers ruffled. Just once."

I gave her a bright non-smile. "Is that why you crept in bed with me? To ruffle my feathers?"

She didn't seem the least bit fazed. "Tell me," she said, twirling her cigarette around with her thumb and finger, "what do you do?"

"What do I do? What do you mean, what do I do?"

"With yourself, I mean. You ever, any time, horsed around? You ever cussed? You ever—even just one time—milked that old mangy cow Etta Klein keeps on the place? I mean, all that reading and longhair record playing, and that sitting in the pavilion house staring at space, I mean, that's not *doing* anything. What's the kick in that? You trying to act like a white boy? Your auntie's right. Old Etta Klein's trying to make a white boy out of you."

I sat down, rather self-consciously straddling a chair. "Really, Della, you certainly have a warped idea of what white boys are like. Just because I don't—"

"Oh, I know what white boys are like, all right." She laughed hoarsely—she did everything hoarsely—and glanced towards the door. "Take him, for instance."

"Who?"

"Jerry. He's so—what do you call it—masculine."

"I suppose."

"He gives me The Nasties."

"The what?"

"The Nasties. I get The Nasties just looking at him. It's not saying I'd *do* anything, even if I got the chance, but he does move me, Lord knows."

"Jerome? Big old fat Jerome? Are you nuts? And anyway, he's white. I thought you said you didn't care for white men."

Della put out her cigarette with a trickle of water from the faucet. "I *never* said that. I just said Etta Klein was making a white boy out of you, and if that's what you want, who gives a damn, Lord knows, I don't. Besides, Jerry isn't really white. He's a Jew."

"Oh, come now, Della. Jews are as white as anything. Whose leg are you pulling?"

Della's eyes widened, to express herself better. "No, silly, I don't mean they're colored or anything like that, but I've been around, and I can tell you Jews aren't white-white. They've got *something* else, I don't know what it is, but it's *something*. I haven't seen a Jew Man yet who didn't move me. And if they're just a tiny bit good-looking, they give me The Nasties like all get out. And I never get The Nasties from just a *plain* white man. And, honey, I know men like I know the palm of my hand."

I didn't know whether to laugh or shout protests. "You're a racist turned inside out, you know that? In your way, you're just as much a bigot as—"

"Horseshit. All you talk is crap you get out of books. You don't know a thing about living, kid, and you never will at the rate you're going. Your soul's going to be white but your skin'll stay black, and Lord help you when you go out into that world out there"—she pointed a long finger towards the acorns and oak trees, out, out, determinedly out where the world was—"where no one'll see how white your soul is. Poor thing. You're so dumb about life it hurts."

I didn't much appreciate Della—Della, Della, amoral Della—lecturing me. "I'd say you have a hell of a lot of learning about life if you think you'll lure Jerome off to bed with you. Such a *sick* idea."

Della dug out another cigarette. "I just said he gives me The Nasties, smarty. That's all I said. Tell me, is this here Maurice LeFleur a Jew?"

There was no reason to think *L'Affaire* LeFleur was a secret after all the ear-splitting histrionics, but his name from her lips startled me. "I haven't the faintest notion what Mr. LeFleur's religion is."

"Horseshit."

"Well, I don't."

"There're a lot of things you don't know, precious. Want old Della Mae to tell you what's what? Want me to tell you what you need?"

"No, thank you."

Della's mouth, laughing, was a ruby hole, pouring out dark contralto.

4

Les Fleurs du mal slid from my knees to the pavilion house floor when I saw him—a big black butterfly pushing his way through Saturday twilight, crunching things underfoot in the grove. One arm flapped in rhythm with the movement of his head, and the other carried a traveling bag. I came out to the edge of the pavilion house and forced my attention through a cluster of sassafras trees, through summer dusk, hoping, in spite of reason, that the ladies had won, that they had burst Jerome's screen of prohibitions. Who else could this man be? I was so certain it was Maurice LeFleur that when he came to the smooth clearing on the lawn, I waved to him, ran to him, extended my hand. "Mr. LeFleur?"

His hand: pale, icy, blue-veined, full of bones, goosefleshed, large appendages to his arms. And his arms were stuffed into a suit of midnight blue. He was of medium height, medium weight, and quite ordinary, except for his head; that was big. And at the top of his big head there was a wide forehead, covered in Hitler fashion with straight inky hair, and the forehead protruded like a canopy over his small black eyes. His nose was Roman, and it hovered, like some proud guardian, over his mouth (which curved in wet Picasso loops), over his watch chain (which curved over his small belly and blue vest), over his patent leather shoes (pointed and full of dew). He was proud of his Roman nose, this Mr. Maurice LeFleur was.

I removed my hand from his and at once became aware that his breath smelled of mint. "I am looking for the lady who owns this place. A Mrs."—he pulled Mrs. Klein's pink stationery (crumpled but clean) from his blue vest pocket— "a Mrs. Etta D. Klein, Green Acorns, Allegan."

"This is the place. Didn't you get a telegram, though? From Kalamazoo? From a Mr. Jerome Klein?"

Maurice LeFleur picked up his bag, of expensive black leather, and marched towards the house. "Several letters. Come. Don't come. Then please come. People hesitate. People are hesitant. I know people. You're Libra aren't you?"

"I'm Oliver. Oh, you mean, yes, Libra. How did you know?"

His small eyes squinted, like a rabbit's. "I just know these things."

Prickly stinging came in waves across my scalp. How could he have known? A wild guess? But when he told Mrs. Klein between spoons of tomato aspic that she was Gemini and just as affirmatively that Aunt Harry was Aries—well, nobody's that good a guesser. He'd done some research . . . yet it was puzzling: Aunt Harry was born in Springfield, Ohio, and I doubted if his research on birth dates had been that thorough. My ladies, however, were convinced, as though the hand of God touched them. Admiration mounted, and so did Maurice LeFleur's cockiness.

"You must be weary, Mr. LeFleur," Aunt Harry said. "We won't keep you up tonight. You can go straight to bed if you want. Room's all nice and ready."

"Northern exposure?" he asked. (There was so much of his *head* sitting at the table.)

Mrs. Klein brightened. "Yes, yes. The best summer breeze in the house."

He folded his napkin and took a toothpick out of his vest pocket. "Oh, I don't know. It might do me harm."

"What might?" Aunt Harry asked.

"Northern exposure."

The ladies conferred, silently, and turned to me. I shook my head furiously: that sonofabitch wasn't going to take *my* room.

Squint-eyed with toothpick rolling over his Picasso lips, he said, "Who was it? Who passed on to the other world? Your relative? Or *your* relative?"

"My son Sargeant. Five years ago."

Maurice LeFleur's blue hand picked up a glass of ice water. "Anything to drink? Any cognac?"

"No, no," Aunt Harry told him, "but some rum. In fact"—the pause was of unkind length—"lots of rum."

"Won't do, won't do. Well, we'll have to get some cognac on Monday, won't we? All right? In fact, there'll be a number of things I might be needing. All right? Now, as for the room, I need to sleep in his bed. A night or two. For contact. All right? I need to have—"

"Oh, but Sargeant never had a room here, Mr. LeFleur. We were living in Kalamazoo for a long time and we were in New York when my son committed—when Sargeant passed away. He—he—"

The ladies gathered themselves: dress-adjusting, turning of rings, crossing their ankles. Aunt Harry said: "We could close the drapes if it's the draft you're worried about. Green Acorns may look old and tumbled down, but the rooms are quite—"

"No, no," he said, his eyes appraising every object in the room, "it should be his bed."

Mrs. Klein was nearly in tears. "But that's impossible, Mr. LeFleur. Sargeant never had a room here. We weren't here when he passed away."

"Well, well, dear lady," he said, not concerned in the least that his hocus-pocus had come to naught, "we'll arrange something, now, won't we? Now, let's see. Your room. I'll need to look at your room for a bit."

"My room?" said Mrs. Klein. "See my room?"

"Yes, yes . . . By the way, I think I'll have a little of that rum if you don't mind . . . and a few of the other rooms, if I may." He drank every drop of the rum down in one swallow. "It's a technical problem. The rooms, I mean. Is it a bother?"

Mrs. Klein was not a selfish woman, but her objects, her things, cluttered in her room, were a comfort to her, a source of security. She lifted her hands to the air, twice, and said, "I guess it's all right. It's really such an old lady's room, Mr. LeFleur. I'm sure if you need to see it for a while I—"

"And you can draw my bath now." This was directed to Aunt Harry, who trembled, drew up her mouth in preparation for a retort that never came. Slowly her pony jaws relaxed, and much of the light of admiration went out of her eyes.

To her rescue, Mrs. Klein said, "Mrs. Gibbs isn't—she isn't exactly—we'll get Della to do it. Della! Della!"

Della was in the room a fraction of a second before she was called. "Will you draw Mr. LeFleur's bath, dear?"

"Draw it?"

"Yes, Della," Aunt Harry said. "You heard her."

"Draw it?"

"Yes, girl," said Aunt Harry. "Just don't stand there like something simple."

"You mean *fix* it, don't you?"

Mrs. Klein glanced at Maurice LeFleur. (It wasn't a glance actually; it was more of a quick sneak over the edge of her handkerchief.) With a certain amount of bite to it, she said to Della, "Why, of course, dear, that's what I mean."

Della spun out of the room but managed to close the door slowly enough for us all to hear her private grievance: "Fix a bath I'll fix, but, Good Lord, I never in my life drawed a bath. . . . You need a dictionary to navigate your way around this . . ."

5

The peacock, the cow, the four chickens, and Bertram (who had an unpronounceable Polish name and was almost totally deaf) knew a stranger was about. Maurice LeFleur dismissed the cow, the chickens, Bertram, but he stood, in the noonday sun in shirtsleeves and vest, dangling a gold chain before the peacock's eyes. It wasn't a very good peacock; it was shabby and timid. In fact, it was mentally disturbed, for it rarely, according to Aunt Harry, had any proud moments.

Maurice asked Bertram its name and Bertram shouted, "Peacock! Peacock!" splitting our ears in two.

"No!" Maurice LeFleur shouted back, "I mean what do you *call* it. What's its name?"

Bertram frowned with anger. "Peacock! Peacock!" he repeated, turning red in the face.

"We just call it 'Peacock,'" I told him, which made Maurice LeFleur ill-tempered for the rest of the day.

Aunt Harry and Mrs. Klein did everything but turn somersaults to amuse him, to coax him back into communication. In fact, they began vying for his attention, almost as though he were a suitor faced with a choice of selecting one or the other to woo. At first I thought my ladies were merely dressing up and putting on their guest manners, but towards the end of the week (Maurice LeFleur was still seeking a "contact point" . . . he was getting closer to Sargeant, he declared at each meal; and each meal, except for lunch, became more rarefied and expensive, much to the dismay of Della and her limited abilities)—but towards the end of the week there was no question that Mrs. Klein and Aunt Harry had gone way beyond the point of hospitality. Mrs. Klein wore her jewels: ruby clips, zircon rings, brooches, earrings of white gold, yellow gold, and once she put on her most prized piece—a cluster of assorted stones shaped in a huge teardrop, which she wore around her neck on a chain. Aunt Harry began to take to powder, usually Mrs. Klein's, which didn't go with her skin; she wore her tea dresses every day, and once I could have sworn she'd plucked a bit of her brows. Had it stopped there, however, I could have chalked it up as mere foolishness, but a pithy bitchiness crept into their conversations with one another; they were getting rough. Too often I was the target, or the funnel through which their frustrated competitiveness ran, and my dubious savior was Maurice LeFleur, whose very entrance into a room soothed their slashing tongues, flooded them with Light and Goodness.

(Della found a friend. I suspected something illicit for several days, but the alliance wasn't, thank God, as grotesque as I at first believed it to be.)

Right after lunch, around two o'clock, Aunt Harry and Mrs. Klein helped each other upstairs, where they took naps until time for rum and tea. I went to the pavilion house where I fingered the pages of *Les Fleurs du mal*, watched bluejays, and worked on my summer poem—to be called "Decipherments & Discontinuities," though I seemed to be renaming it every other week. Thirst finally brought me to the kitchen for a beer, and there in the steamy kitchen I found Maurice LeFleur with his shirt open to the belly button, fanning his sweating face, smoking a thin little cigar. Della was saying, "If you think I'm going to Kansas City to make blue movies, you've got another think coming."

"You don't have to. Anyway, Chicago's better. A colored gal in Chicago can make a fistful of dough. All you got to do, baby, is to—" The nearest thing to a blush he could manage spread over his face when he saw me. Della turned, wondering what had stopped him, and then she giggled. Hoarsely. "Go ahead, Maurie, it's only Oliver. Did you know Oliver's a virgin?"

He stopped fanning and weighed the merit of her remark for a second or two. "I've got some stuff that's a very good stimulant. I could sell it to you for next to nothing."

"You can keep it. All I want is a beer."

Della's hands pushed the refrigerator door shut in my face. "Did you know Oliver's groomin' to be a white boy? Our little precious-precious Oliver?"

"For crying out loud, Della, will you let me get some beer, or won't you?"

"All gone. There's cognac and God knows there's rum. Wanna little rum?"

"No."

Maurice LeFleur stopped fanning again. "Let's have a Daiquiri, huh? Fix some Daiquiris, Della."

"How? *You* fix it, Maurie. I never made one of them drinks in my life."

So we had Daiquiris in the kitchen, and our tongues grew thick, while the bees ran through the afternoon air and my ladies upstairs slept. Maurice LeFleur bit crushed ice and held his cocktail close to his Roman nose. "You really a virgin, kid?" he asked suddenly, breaking into the silence and the sound of bees.

"Ask Della. She's the authority on that."

Della was pretty tight, and the lids of her big hazel eyes had a hard time rising and falling. "Ha, he's scared shitless of women. A couple of weeks ago he was terrified out of his mind when I came in his room. Poor thing, nearly had a stroke."

Both of them were across the table from me, the drunken inquisitor and inquisitress. "I told you then, like I'm telling you now, A, I thought it was PG; and B, I was sound asleep. I don't know about you, but I can't jump from one emotional state to another—"

"Get that talk, Maurie. 'Emotional state.' Ain't it the kicks?"

"And C, even if I *was* awake and *knew* it wasn't PG, I don't happen to find you the least bit attractive—I mean, for me."

"I'm that bad, huh?"

"For *me,* yes. For somebody else you might be heaven, for Christ's sake." Maurice LeFleur didn't react one way or the other; he was just staring at me. Then he said: "How much is that old lady spending on you? At that school and all?"

"Enough. Why?"

"How much?"

"Enough. What business is it of yours? I mean, enough is enough, isn't it?"

Della breathed down his neck with an intimacy. "The works, Maurie. I told you Etta Klein is stinky-pie rich. If it gave her a thrill, she could afford to burn ten-dollar bills."

He kept looking at me, with a toothpick on his wet lips. "You're a mighty fortunate kid, you know that? She going to leave you any money when she goes on to the Hereafter?"

When he said "Hereafter," the goddamned charlatan wouldn't even fake it enough to take the toothpick out of his mouth. I got up. "Your interest in money is inordinate, and, I'm afraid, a bit vulgar. Excuse me, I'm going back to the yard."

"Get off my back, kid. Your kind of game, it doesn't hoodwink me a bit."

With disdain and hauteur (though the image was perhaps marred somewhat by my drunkenness) I walked from the kitchen, dropping bits of Baudelaire (*mon coeur est un palais flétri par la cohue*) on the rabble who sought to demean me.

TWO

1

At midnight I heard him molesting Peacock. The view of
the backyard from my window was smeared with moon
shadows, and it was a limited view; it was not at all possible
to be certain just what he was up to by peeking out at the
lawn. It was entirely too melodramatic, this rustling in
the night, and because nothing would awaken Bertram
except the coming of 5 a.m., I felt it my responsibility to go
down to the backyard and make a check. It was, of course,
curiosity and distrust that prompted me to investigate less
forthrightly (i.e., tiptoeing in the dark) than the situation
demanded.

I stood there in a shadow, listening. The night was alive
with small things in the grass and with moving vans rolling towards Chicago on the highway a couple of miles
away. My surreptitious stance behind the hothouse wall
(as though I were in a wax museum), waiting for Maurice
LeFleur to commit some outrage, became, little by little,
embarrassing: suppose I had not really heard him and he
was, that very minute, cradling his earthenware head in a
blissful snore! Dreaming, maybe, of warlocks! That image,

though, was replaced immediately with the real one: there he was, hardly twenty feet away, lugging a small ladder at his side. As he passed I could have touched him, and then he walked to the west side of the house, the side where the pavilion house sat in the distance on the lawn, and he placed the ladder above the music room window. The summer moon burned down almost without interruption; the only shadows were the ones that hugged the far edges of the lawn, except the one shadow, tall and slender, that came from the pavilion house. It was, therefore, difficult to watch him undetected. Once, as I peeked around the corniced edge of the house, my shadow spilled over the grass like great leaks of ink. Again I tried, without looking at my leaping shadow, and I saw that he was far too involved in his struggle up the lattice work, cornices, gazebo designs, and gingerbread filigree to see shadows or to see me. He'd left the ladder, climbed above the first floor level, and began testing his foothold on a half-foot ridge that surrounded the second story. He stood there on the ridge, in the light of the moon, in shirtsleeves and vest, with his gold chain dangling.

By this time I'd come out in the open; I was standing directly behind the ladder, looking up at him, but he still didn't see me. Quietly he edged along the small ridge, touching and testing the strength of pieces of the house as he went along, and he paused a bit in front of Mrs. Klein's window, twisting his head in some private quandary, and then nodded to himself up there, high up there on the ledge. He seemed satisfied as he came down the ladder, his patent leather heels kicking outwards into the moonlight as he—like a butterfly in a vest—descended. I retreated into a shadow as he passed by with the orange glow of his cigar end leading his way.

But it was a sloppy crime, if it were really a crime, his wallscaling: he'd left the ladder leaning on the side of the house. Bertram would surely see it the first thing in the morning.

But what was the purpose of all that stealthy stuff in the night?

Our house-thief-in-residence was spooning a pear when Bertram came up to the breakfast table and told us in heavy Polish accents about the ladder he found near the music room window.

"Oh, now, now, Bertram," Mrs. Klein said over her tea, and smiled at Maurice LeFleur. The smile across the table was tantamount to reaching out and patting Bertram on the head, as one might do to a tiresome child. Bertram, of course, was furious: he might have been as deaf as a doorknob, but absent-minded he was not. He avenged his ignominy at the breakfast table with some words in Polish, probably dirty, and scuffed smartly off to tend Peacock and the cow.

Aunt Harry made a big thing over buttering her muffin and said, just before she took a bite, "It'd be a good thing anyway, Etta, if you put more locks on your jewels."

I thought her little fat fingers would snap the tea cup handle. "Oh, hush, Harriet Gibbs. I don't need you to start telling me what to do with my jewels."

"A word to the wise," she said with so much ice that it seemed she'd originated the adage right on the spot.

After considerable silence, Mrs. Klein tapped her fingers on the linen towards Aunt Harry's direction. "Nobody in his right mind would come all the way out to Green Acorns to take old lady things. Bertram's just getting forgetful and old like the rest of us and he doesn't want to admit it."

Then, after *another* considerable silence (had it taken so long to think of a retort?), Aunt Harry said, as though she'd just made a move in a chess game, "Well, there's a first time for everything."

With a Dramatic Academy ruffle of sleeves, Mrs. Klein raised her arms to press her cheeks with her hands, and as she leaned towards Maurice LeFleur she said, "Dear Harriet's riddled with clichés this morning, isn't she, Mr. LeFleur?"

In the bright light of morning, Maurice LeFleur looked very much like a crook. How could I have believed for a second that his moonlight business was in any way romantic? Also, as the sunlight beat across the porcelain and orange juice and linen and silverware, my loyalty was revived, and by the end of breakfast it had grown so vigorously that I announced I was taking a trip into Kalamazoo.

"Really, dear boy?" Mrs. Klein touched my arm, but she hadn't heard; her mind was involved with watching Maurice LeFleur's decadent style of lighting his tiny cigar.

Aunt Harry pointed a finger at me and snapped it back. "Now listen, I want you back here before it gets dark, understand? We don't want to have to worry ourselves sick like we did last week." Seated, tall-backed, she stacked the table's dishes, moving her fiberglass hair above the linen in the sunlight. "I don't know why you have to hightail it over to Kalamazoo to see movies. They all come right here to Allegan sooner or later. What bus you getting?"

"One-fifteen, I guess."

Maurice LeFleur, through smoke and sunlight, kept his voice at a breakfast-table pitch. "You going to Kalamazoo?"

I thought I heard his pulse beating. "Yeah. To see a movie. To mess around."

"What movie?" His eyes darted like hornets. They were stinging my face.

"Huh, it's—"

"And listen, young man," Aunt Harry broke in, "be sure you have clean underwear on. I don't expect it to happen, God forbid, but if you got into an accident, and they had to take you to the hospital, and you had on dirty underwear, I'd be mortified to an inch of my life." Before she went to the kitchen to give Della instructions, she turned, with a handful of egg-smeared dishes, and said, "And change your socks, too."

It was three-fifteen when I got to Jerome's house. It was still too early to expect to find him at home, but I was impatient and burning with a mission, and there was nothing to do in Kalamazoo in the middle of the afternoon. The long driveway up to the lawn was lined with slender evergreens, spaced in picture book dullness, and the grass, rolling uphill and downhill at the side of the drive, seemed as though it had been pampered under a spyglass: not a blade was out of place. Ground sprinklers twisted and turned in exotic arabesques, and the water, white-silver, spewed into the air and fell in tricky choreography. The big fat limousine wasn't in the garage, but the tiny red Fiat sat there sparkling like a store window toy.

I'd expected Jerome's snotty butler to answer the bell, but I heard heel-clicking down the marble foyer; it was, with a strand of pearls and in a raspberry dress, Patricia Jo Klein née Walker who opened the door.

"My goodness! Oliver! Anything wrong?" She fingered her pearls and stood there staring at me.

"Hello. No. Not exactly. I'm too early for Jerome, I suppose."

She laughed and showed teeth as regular, as white, as cold, as her pearls. "My goodness, yes. He went down to Saint Louis for the day"; and with a shrill jerk of her hand (nails raspberry color, too) she said, "Well, goodness, come in." She turned away towards the drawing room, clicking her heels as though there was no doubt who was the mistress of the house. "Come in, come in. Anything wrong?"

I sat across from Jerome's wife. She was tall. Her hair looked enormously beauty parlored, but it had, for all of its intricacy of design, a good measure of dowdiness. If she had beauty, it was a cautious and polite beauty; and if it was not beauty she had, then her plainness was expensively disguised. What Jerome saw in her twenty years ago when he was courting was not easily discernible, for even in the most concentrated conjuring it was impossible to bring forth images of her indulging in ardor, necking in a car seat, being clandestine—as Aunt Harry and Mrs. Klein had often hinted. For one thing, her mouth was all wrong for ardor: it was such a severe red line—a cut, really, across her powdered face. The middle of her lips were perpetually puckered, as though she were about to say something in French. And for another thing, she didn't have much neck. She was tall and slender, but after her shoulders her head came, suddenly, without enough preparation. Yet she wasn't a truly ugly woman. It just seemed that she should have been teaching geometry in Kalamazoo Central High School instead of being an idle Gracious Lady. More than anything, though, she was awfully short on *esprit de corps*; she relaxed behind expensive clothes and decorum, as though that were enough, as though both her clothes and her decorum could hide all inadequacies. In short, she put entirely too much trust in tangible camouflage, a bad habit she perhaps picked up from her working days. Mrs. Klein once said she'd been a secretary at Klein Stove Manufacturers—"in some low capacity, my dear, and she slept her way right up to my son." But that always struck me as unlikely; she hadn't nearly enough *esprit*, and virgin was written all the way across her face. I, for one, am sure she would have had her twin boys immaculately had it at all been possible. No, it was unthinkable that she succeeded at KSM by offering treasures in the boudoir. Her ankles were big, too. Her feet were rather small. And she had football-playing hips. Although her breasts were ample, there was hardly any delineation to speak of—they weren't low and dumpy and peasantlike, but they certainly weren't the kind a woman in her right mind would ever stick into a sweater. Well . . . Jerome wasn't a beauty either, and he probably took a wife in the same pragmatic way he took over his father's business. On the other hand, perhaps it had been most romantic; perhaps there'd been an Abélard and Héloïse flair, a Tristan and Isolde intensity, a Romeo and Juliet—in fact, a Romeo and Julietism Aunt Harry had tried more than once to assign their liaison. But for the life of me I could never see how anyone could be passionate

With a little black bag. And his name is Maurice LeFleur."
I paused but she didn't interject anything this time, so
I said, "He reads palms, cups, astrological charts, cards,
gives séances, and probably steals jewelry. It's the robbing
I'm worried about. There's one piece in particular that—"

"Yes, I know. A lovely piece. And Mother Klein won't
insure it, won't protect it. And the thing is, she rarely wears
it. It's a pity, too. A lovely piece."

I didn't think it was all that lovely. Expensive, perhaps, but aesthetically quite tawdry. It was an assortment
of costly stones shaped into a form of an immense drop
of water, or a tear, and it looked very much like something Hansel and Gretel might well have plucked from
the witch's house to eat.

"But, Oliver," she was saying, "why did they ask this
man to come out? This type—what is he there for?"

"Jerome was against it, but he's there all the same—this
Maurice LeFleur. I think they just want company, some
excitement, really, but they say he's there to give a séance.
And he's not a bad sort—in a way."

Her teeth were showing but she soon covered them
with lips that seemed ready to pronounce *puissance*, or
pleur, or something. "A séance? Oh, now, that's just too
much nonsense. Why a séance?"

"To bring Sargeant back. To communicate with
Sargeant."

I should have been careful; I should have led into mention of Sargeant gently; his name always, inexplicably,
made her pallor go bad. She drew her small feet back a bit,
together, and they stood there, half under the settee. They
looked very lonely.

"But that's ridiculous. Why should they do a thing like that? Mother Klein's got Jerome—and Harriet has, too, in a way. They've got Jerome. Why should they do a thing so demented? Oh, I've told Jerome a hundred times, at least a hundred times, that he should do something with Mother Klein. Letting her stay out there alone, living in— well, nearly alone—you must admit your aunt is nearly as peculiar as Jerome's mother is. They're both too old to be living in such a—a bizarre sort of circumstance. At least a nursemaid, I say. At least that concession. It's—"

"A nursemaid? Are you kidding? They'd—both of them—shoot a nursemaid dead with a forty-five before she unpacked. They aren't senile, you know."

I'm afraid my tone was sharp and Patricia Jo, I knew so well, didn't like sharp tones; long ago she'd gotten rid of all of Jerome's sharp tones. So it didn't surprise me when she said, pinching her lips so that they nearly disappeared altogether, "I know quite well Mother Klein's capabilities, and your aunt's too, for that matter. There're certain things in life you just have to put up with, and the sooner they learn this the better. I simply can't convince Jerome. I do honestly think sometimes he is afraid of Mother Klein. I honestly think this. I've told him over and over Green Acorns is too far from Allegan for two old ladies and a feeble-minded yard attendant—or whatever that insolent Polish man is—too far out for them to live. Suppose—"

"It's only a mile and a half from the heart of town and the nearest neighbor is just twenty minutes away. Less actually."

She would have slapped me had I been her child and within reach. "A mile and a half to what? A dinky third-rate hospital? And who are the neighbors? That tacky *nouveau riche* Belle Thompson and her roué brothers. It's a dirty joke to even mention their names." Her hands flew up from the Louis Quinze and made fist clinches in the air, a gesture that seemed monstrously dramatic and not at all suitable for her metabolism. "Oh, what I'm trying to say is—Suppose Mother Klein, or your aunt, had a heart attack—and you know full well your aunt's heart is in a bad condition—or suppose the house caught fire, or heaven knows what!"

I sat there and waited to see if there was any more venom coming up, and then I told her, in tones calculated to indicate my *Weltanschauung* was to be reckoned with, "But they can't stop living and making wild concessions simply because they're getting older. All life's a risk. It's merely a greater risk as one gets older." This was almost a verbatim quote from Benson—a tutor I once had—but, unfortunately, it was a mistake, for her tongue lashed out from behind her cruel lips and her mouse eyes came to life.

"What do you know about it? *What* exactly? Don't you know it's bad even for you—being out there—being brought up by two half—half—Two old ladies and tutor after tutor after tutor? It's unhealthy that hothouse atmosphere, Oliver. It's unreal. You're going to suffocate or grow so impossibly precious that—" Oh, Lord! There was that word again. Precious! Precious! She talked on and I could see the red slit in her face as she lectured, but my brain hung on "precious" and it flared up and stung me and kept me from hearing anything else. Della had said it and now *she* had said it; it had a hissing sound when they said it, and it seemed too strong for anything to kill it. ". . . of course, we're all certain that, academically, you'll do extremely well, but goodness, what a problem it's going to be for you to adjust. You haven't learned to—to recognize that you're to—" My gaze, which was no doubt feverish, made her falter. "To cope," she ended, struggling for breath and thankful she'd come to a respectable coda.

I sat there bleeding. It had been her round. And then, crossing my legs, I lit one of Mrs. Klein's English Ovals. I extinguished the flaming match without removing the cigarette from my mouth, and very gently, but with ferocious sureness, exhaled through my nose to make doubly sure she would not miss my smoking expertise. Apparently the shock numbed her, but, more logically, I was seventeen (almost) and I was leaving home to go to college, so perhaps she thought better about commenting upon my nicotine vice. "I suppose, Mrs. Klein," (I'd never gotten around to calling her Patricia Jo to her face and it seemed now the least likely time to attempt it) "you're right—to some extent perhaps—but we've all our fortes and our faults, haven't we? Actually, I'm fairly moderate in my vices, and it's not being immodest when I say that scholastically I excel."

She whinnied. Briefly. But it was a whinny, for she put a raspberry nail to her lips to hide it. My rapier had touched its mark: moderate in his vices, her son Mark was not. Twice he was nearly ousted from Harvard for drunkenness in public places, and it was rumored he drank heavily behind closed doors alone. Marcus, her other son, had been called during various stages of his life cute, sweet, handsome, a good guy, a Regular Joe, but bright, even the most charitable had never pronounced him.

"I really must go. Almost immediately. Anything you want me to tell Jerome?"

"No. Except LeFleur is there. Kissing petticoats and planning plunder. The séance part will probably fizzle out. Who knows. Anyway, he hasn't the least notion why Sargeant committed suicide. It's this Saturday, I think."

She turned the color of Bertram's roses. "Is *that* why they want to have it? To find out *why* he did it? Oh. Oh, I see."

She lifted her face a bit, in a vague frown (yet a piece of a smile appeared, too), and looked towards the big clock in the hallway. "Oh, I see," she said again, her head turning on her shoulders, slowly. "We *shall* have some drink, Oliver. A little mild sherry, hmm? You must tell me about this Maurice LeFleur. Lorenzo! Lorenzo! Excuse me. Lorenzo!" She went to the hall to tell her snotty butler to bring in some sherry.

The sherry was nutty, full-bodied. It was a shame the bribe was so exquisite; there was nothing to tell except what LeFleur looked like, what I thought he might do, but I labored through miniscule descriptions anyway, fearing she would snatch away the sherry out of disappointment.

I started on another sherry and asked with all the urbanity I could muster, "You don't believe in séances, do you?"

Her mouse eyes were still burning and she couldn't keep her fingers still. "Of course I don't, of course I don't." I could hear her breathing clear across the table, and then she asked, "And he plans to tell *why*? Why Sargeant did it?" As she asked the question her eyes began crisscross flights around the room. "Oh, goodness," she said, "what a mess."

What-a-mess turned out to be a slight and barely notice-able slant in the short drapes over two tiny windows above a mantle ridge. She hauled over a straightback chair, as though her task were the most important thing in the world, and sat it beneath the mantle and the drapes. Her foot was almost on top of the chair before she thought better of standing on it unprotected, and retracted it, that small foot hooked on to the big ankle. "Oliver, take off your shoes and come over here to hold this drapery rod." She surprised herself, I sus-pect, with her imperious command, so she added, with sugar and spice, "Won't you be a dear?"

Thank God for old crabby Aunt Harry! My socks were clean! They usually had, I must admit, a tendency to be sweaty in the summertime.

Patricia Jo handed me a little silver pencil she pulled out from an antique-looking escritoire and had me lift and lower, lift and lower—God, it went on for eternity—the drapery rod to the exact spot it was to be marked.

"You can't really trust anybody anymore. If you want something done correctly, you—no, no, that's *too* high now, Oliver. Down just a fraction of a fraction."

A fraction of a fraction, of course, is all in the behold-er's mind; scientifically, this vivid designation cannot be calculated, particularly when one is at nose length with the damned problem. "More, more," she nagged from below, and it was at this point, I think—although I'm not pre-pared to admit that I was consciously malicious—I gave it much more than a fraction of a fraction. "Oh, for goodness' sake," she said, kicking off her shoes, "let me get up there."

Now it may seem a very simple thing, but I'm sure she didn't realize that her new vantage point—nose and head two inches from the faulty rod—placed her at a distinct disadvantage. She shifted the rod, which was surprisingly heavy, up and down gingerly, but she now had to ask me if it was even, and as soon as she asked she realized how disastrous our change of position was: she had to depend upon *my* judgment. I stood there in the middle of her living room basking in the irony of the whole Marx Brothers escapade, and the enjoyment must have shown from my face, for as she turned her head (straight from the shoulders) and looked at me her arms trembled, partly, I dare say, from the weight of the rod, but largely from sheer rage. And that's when the freakish accident occurred. Just about at that moment.

As her arms trembled above her head, which was turned towards me, the rod slipped from her fingers pulling the secure end from its fastener on the wall. She tried valiantly to grab the rod, the drapes, as they tumbled down, but the chair position was too close, and it seemed she did not dare too much movement for fear it would topple over. Butterfingers Patricia Jo Klein missed everything, rod and all. This might have been merely a domestic *divertissement* in the afternoon had it not been for the tiny prongs on the end of the rod. Somehow as the rod tumbled to the floor it snagged her stocking at the knee, leaving an ugly spurt of blood and pulling the stocking down, down over the calf of the leg, where it ended in a pool around her ankle. It was cruel misfortune, that pool of stocking around her ankle, for the stocking surrounded it in such a—a—well, it was so irrevocable, that act of her stocking. I never knew before that an inanimate object could be so impertinent, so petulant, so grandly hideous. Its silence spoke now—hushed in that flabby nylon pile around her ankle and foot. To me, and I'm sure to her, the blood at her knee was remarkably insignificant; it was that pool of nylon that froze our stares.

And now a confession: I've done two highly dis-honorable things in my life. I don't think they are funny, I don't think they're clever, and I'm not at all proud of these acts of infamy. Once on a windy March I was wait-ing in line at the Bijou to see Katharine Hepburn in a movie, and a ticket intended for a frail old man blew out from the ticket window and stuck to the leather of my jacket. I secured the ticket, covering it with my glove, but stood in my tracks watching the old man scamper around, nearly on hands and knees, searching for his lost ticket. I shamelessly clung to the ticket, even as he whispered and pawed his way around the feet of the queue. Selfishly I could only think of the cigarettes I could buy with the movie money I would save. It was two years ago, at a time had I been caught smoking Aunt Harry would have used Chinese torture as a punishment, and it was during those months the doctor forbade Mrs. Klein to smoke or to use rum (but, God knows, rum flowed on). My allowance was used up and Benson refused to lend me even a nickel. (He was a cheap bastard; I've always hated him for that. He could say marvelous-sounding things about The Nature of Generosity, but he couldn't for a minute put this theo-rem into practice.) Anyway, it was to be a desperate three days without cigarettes, for Hepburn had won out over my nicotine desires. I'd intended to be strong about it; I'd see Hepburn and suffer, but when the ticket—and, oh, I rationalized it as being an Act of God—popped smack into me, I would not let the pathetic little man's frenzy unbend me. As it turned out, I didn't enjoy the movie one bit, not because of Hepburn (she could have been in a Hawaiian travelogue for all I cared), but guilt prodded me so much that I looked right and left all during the movie to see if I could find the little man I'd robbed, to see if the stern, overpowdered ticketseller had given him another ticket. For nights I dreamed of craggly hands and darkened movie houses.

My second Dishonorable Deed was no less profane. Alas, cigarettes again. I cannot remember the reason I had no money, for it was summer and I made extra change by reading Shakespeare sonnets to Belle Thompson during the time she was convalescing with a foot infection. (This was before Belle Thompson got rich on a sweepstake ticket and got bawdy and her roué brothers came all the way from Detroit to live with her. Also, this was before her attitude towards Shakespeare changed.) Nevertheless I was broke, and although Mrs. Klein was smoking English Ovals like winter chimneys, and packages were easy to pilfer (and I suspect she knows, has known all along, I steal her cigarettes—I've seen her "place" them in spots I would likely come upon—I do think it's another cross-purposing of Aunt Harry that instigates her to do this), I was greedy and wanted to buy a whole carton. *My first whole carton.* Anyway, I used Mother's Day money to buy the carton. Not English Ovals; I'd smoke anything those days. So for a Mother's Day present—always for both Aunt Harry and Mrs. Klein—I stole flowers from the cemetery. There was nothing macabre about it, really; I took them in broad daylight, on a warm May Sunday. Somebody had been recently buried and there were hundreds of fresh, expensive, multicolored blooms spread over a rich mound of sand. From them I made two enormous bouquets, one for each. I did pray that night, I think, that the corpse would forgive me. . . .

And now I was about to perform my third Dishonorable Deed. I didn't want to—or at least I kept telling myself that—but it was dishonorable, indeed, to stand there staring at that pool of stocking at Patricia Jo's ankle and allowing her to see a smile light up my face. My smile felt, as it grew across my chin, victorious. A snicker would have been far more preferable, but, no, I gave in to impulse and stood there, head slightly bent towards her disgrace, giving forth a Victory Smile.

I must give Patricia Jo credit, though: when she started crying, there was no pretense that it was for her cut knee; that would have been too womanly, too weak. It has a plain open howl, a kind of defeat, and as it continued, I began to admire her for being strong, for having the nerve to cry like that with such open admission. Although it clipped my victory considerably, my estimation of her *esprit* rose to a point that almost made me like her. And after—oh, it seemed like ten minutes, her no-neck face crying on top of the chair—after a time I walked across the room with my handkerchief and pressed away some of the trickling blood. I'd fully expected her to slap me for this; I think probably I wanted her to; I think probably I was seeking punishment for my dishonorable gloating. At least it would have evened the score again, for I was at that moment way ahead. But instead she placed her raspberry nails on my shoulders, came down from the chair, sat on it, and cried even harder into my seersucker jacket. She clawed my backbone and soiled me with tears, mascara, and lipstick.

"Oh, Oliver," she cried, straight into my belly, "my marriage isn't good. It isn't good, it isn't good, it isn't."

I looked at the drying blood in the handkerchief in my hand. I looked at three gray hairs on the top of her head. I looked up at the window, which had caused all the fuss. Then, rather quickly, she pulled her face away and turned in the chair. "It isn't thoroughly rotten," she said, taking the handkerchief away from me, "but it's bad enough," and she told me in sniveling torrents the Story of Her Life, or at least the part concerned with her not being Jewish and Jerome being Jewish and the difficulties with in-laws. Her monologue was studded with sociological-sounding words like "society" and "conformity" and "group pressure" and God knows what all. It would have made quite a nice radio serial.

I started to say something pertinent about the shaky props of decorum, but I'd begun to like her—how can you *not* like someone who crys into your belly!—and it was right at that second she looked up with her drab brown eyes and disarmed me. "You know, I hated you when you walked in that door earlier—I've always hated you—oh, no, I guess, not that strong . . . but you were, in an odd way, always being Sargeant to Mother Klein. Jerome, Jerome never . . . never . . . well, I do like you after all." Then she turned away to stare across to the settee. "But, Oliver, I hate myself, I think. Hate myself for being such a coward . . . with Jerome's mother. And—and I always wonder if Jerome thinks it is my fault, if— Really, it's awful sometimes. Sometimes it is awful . . ."

My position was awkward; I didn't know if I was supposed to contribute to the proceedings or not. It seemed too much of a nervous monologue too long stifled, and now that it had begun, it seemed brutish to interfere. But it all ended with silence, a silence that finally became insulting; I would not stand there, tear-soaked, in the middle of her drawing room all afternoon while she thought red-eyed thoughts about the state of her marriage. But finally she snapped out of it, and said, "That man who's out there, Oliver, what's his name?"

"LeFleur. Maurice LeFleur."

"Yes. That LeFleur man. Who knows. He might not be—the idea might not be so crazy after all."

"How do you mean?"

"I mean, as long as Mother Klein has this Sargeant ghost hanging about, Jerome will never be her son. Never. I know that. It's that simple. Don't you see that?" She took off the torn stocking and stood up. Then she sat back down, fingering the snag in the stocking. "Don't you see that? Nobody escapes. Even you. In fact—she's practically training *you* to be Sargeant. More or less. Don't you see that?"

Patricia Jo née Walker Klein stood up and pressed her raspberry nails to her eye sockets. "You're probably laughing, aren't you? That I'm making too much of this, that I'm being—" She threw her hands into the air in a flight of raspberry desperation. "All I know is since Sargeant's suicide things have not been the same. Not that they were so red-hot before. More sherry?"

"No, thanks. No, yes I will."

She began pampering the room again, and in the middle of her floral adjustment I said, for the second time that afternoon, "You believe in séances, don't you?"

"No, not necessarily. No, I don't."

"But you *must*. Otherwise—"

"Otherwise I'd ask Jerome to put a stop to it. Right?"

"Right."

"No, Oliver. I'm clutching at straws, I suppose. I don't believe in those things, but people must get *something* out of them, some satisfaction. So what's the harm—as long as you get the jewelry locked up?"

"But you believe a little bit. Don't you?"

"When you get older"—and before she finished I wanted to protest; I was pretty sick of that old chestnut, dropped by the aged (Benson, Aunt Harry, and now Patricia Jo) whenever they were in a tight spot; it was a dirty ploy, this more-experienced-than-thou weapon used by elders to win the game when they were losing—"you'll understand that one has to believe a little bit in almost everything."

I was again afraid to speak for fear I'd destroy our new-found rapport.

"Now! This time," she announced, advancing towards the drapes on the floor, "we'll do it sensibly. Come!"

As much as I admired her resilience, I could not help feeling a bit disgusted with her: there was no point of being so aggressively athletic on top of all that expenditure of emotion. "You're going to try to put these up again?"

She'd already gathered the drapes from the floor. "I don't see any reason why not." The cut-mouth look was regaining prominence in her face and fire came again to her mouse eyes.

It was sheer inspiration on my part to remember her tea engagement. "But I thought you had an appointment soon," I said, solicitous as hell.

"Oh, God!" She dropped the drapes, right where she'd picked them up, and grabbed her shoes. "Wait here. I won't be long. I'll drop you off at the station."

Two small sherries later she came back to the room with her new face, with some white gloves, a purse and a hat. It was off-putting, that face; it was exactly the same as it'd been when I arrived. It was amazing: cosmetics on her face were better than liters of adrenalin in the blood. Twice, as we rolled down the wooded drive on the way towards South Street—and her tiny Fiat wasn't red; it was more raspberry, the color of her dress—I turned to look at her face to see if there was any sign of Patricia Jo, the woman I'd briefly seen; there was only the confident glow of her cosmetic armor.

She drove down South Street to see how many cars had arrived at the house in which she was to have her tea, and then drove me on to the Greyhound Station. "I suppose you have your ticket. Money to get back."

"Yes, thanks."

I had one leg out of the car when she asked, "When is the night of the séance?"

"This Saturday, I imagine. You—you're not going to tell Jerome?"

"I think not."

2

At dusk I came back to Green Acorns, via the kitchen, to find that Della was about to have an attack of The Nasties. I could tell by her eyes. And those hazel eyes of hers caught right away the mess on the front of my jacket. (The soap and water in the Men's Room at the Greyhound Station had only exaggerated the disaster.)

"I hope you done ate," she said, washing a dish painfully, "cause there ain't a thing left."

"I'll make a sandwich."

"No, you won't. I don't want you messing around in my frige. It's bad enough with Maurie and Mrs. K and your auntie. There's too much traffic in that frige as it is. You look for the butter and it's down with the—sit, I'll fix it. You like cold tongue? If you don't it's tough titty cause that's all there is." Her hands were still sudsy as she pulled out accouterments to make a sandwich. "You look for the lettuce and it's behind the milk. Lord, I can't wait to take off from this place. Wasting my youth," she said, glaring down at her mammalian appendages, "in this nut house.

And what's wrong with your jacket? Looks like you been doing something lewd."

"Where are you going to take off to? Kansas City to make blue movies?"

She slapped salad dressing on the tongue sandwich with bravura and with a fascinating inefficiency. "Don't change the subject, smarty-pants. What's all that mess on your jacket? Where you been?"

I couldn't wait to get into the sandwich, but, no, she had to be fancy and cut it into genteel little pieces.

"Well?"

"To a house of ill repute, maybe."

She threw her head back and her gold tooth showed. "Ha. That'll be the day. There'll be dancing in the street and papers will make big headlines of it. There'll be—"

"Oh, shut up, Della, for crying out loud."

"Listen, don't get smart with me. Your little uppity white boy ways don't cut any ice with me. You make me sick. And you're heading for a downfall, just as sure as—"

"Good gravy, we're back at that again, I see. Got any soda?"

"There's some filthy punch we had for supper," she said, returning to the sink. "Get it yourself."

"I thought you didn't want anybody messing around in your refrigera—"

"I said get it yourself."

"All right, all right. I just thought—"

"Get it yourself, Oliver Eugene! Damnit, don't tax me. I'm in no mood for it. You hear me?"

"La, la. You *are* in a state, aren't you, old girl?"

"I'm warning you, Oliver, don't be smart with me. I'm in no mood for it. You hear me?"

I began eating in silence and that killed her, too. "Damn," she said softly, pouring hot water over the soapy dishes. Then she dried her hands and reached on top of her breadbox for her cigarettes. "Maurie came out here a little bit ago and gave me The Nasties something awful." She drew on her cigarette so hard that the hollows of her cheeks sank in.

"You and Maurice LeFleur?"

"Not him, not him. He don't do a thing for me. Not if we was Adam and Eve, for chrissake. But he had all this talk about Chicago and how great it was and how I could have a ball almost anytime I wanted and how—"

"Really, don't you ever think about anything besides sex?"

"Don't you *ever* think about it? You're just like Sargeant. Your head's in the clouds."

"Now stop that lie! You didn't even know Sargeant, and you know it."

"Well, I hear talk."

"What kind of talk? From whom?"

"Your auntie and Mrs. K. Those two go on night and day. Picking that poor man apart. He sure must be twisting in his grave."

"Oh, you listen, huh?"

"Christ, you can't help it. And now that Maurie needs to know stuff for his séance, I just listen closer, that's all." She sat down at the table across from me and smelled the punch. "Slop," she said, wincing, and in a glittering, conspiratorial stutter she said, "I'm going off with him. I'm going to run off with him and I'll break your neck if you tell." Her excitement was too great for her to sit still; she made a big to-do with crossing and uncrossing her turkey legs at the side of the table. "He knows lots of people. Lots of contact. He can set me up, start me off." She threw her arms up over her head—knocking askew her maid's cap as she did it—and laughed. Hoarsely. "Bye-bye dirty dishes and scrubbing and cleaning up white folks' scraps. Della Mae is going to be free, honey. She's going to live while livin' is still good."

"Are you sure he's not pulling your leg, Della?"

She lit another cigarette, rather mannishly, and said, "We're thick, us two. It's tit for tat. I help him, he helps me."

"With dubious information concerning Sargeant, I take it."

"Sort of. And other things." And with a cheap imitation of a character from one of her bedtime books (*The Sailor's Mistress*, *Sally's Saloon*, etc.), she said, "I'm not at liberty to divulge."

It was wiser to wash down the cold tongue with punch than to probe further; her *idée fixe*, obviously, was there to stay. "Where's everybody?" I asked, taking the last of Mrs. Klein's English Ovals from my jacket.

"Christ knows. Out at the pavilion house playing with Peacock, I think. Say, you know something? I think both those old gals are in love with Maurie."

"Nonsense."

"Hey!" She scooped up the empty cigarette package and dumped it in the trash. "You want Mrs. K to think that I'm the one who's been pinching her cigarettes? No, what I mean is, not *that* kind of love, silly. But they fight over him. Like little old schoolgirls."

"He's company for them," I offered.

She was impatient and took my punch glass to the sink. "Christ, you're always trying to put some meaning to things, just like that Goon Head Finley Benson. I'm not saying if he's company for them or not; I'm saying they're in love with him." And to fully satisfy her retort, she tacked on: "You always know so damned much."

"Well," I said, getting up, "things are like that, I guess."

"Don't you be flip with me. One thing I can't stand is for somebody to be flip all the time or for somebody to signify."

"Signify? What's 'signify'?"

"Signifyin'"—she laughed in contralto and dried her hands—"signifyin' is worse than lyin'. You wouldn't know what that means with that white soul of yours. You been away from the race too long, kid. That's something you just automatically know."

I dumped ashes in her sink and told her she was a racist. "It's all environmental conditioning. If a person is brought up—"

"Horseshit."

(All her arguments, when backed into the wall, ended with that singularly vulgar comment.)

I was about to leave but she stopped me. "Come here and let me get that stuff off your jacket before your auntie sees it and has a conniption. My nerves can't stand no conniption this evening. Especially from that woman. Come here. What is it?"

I came back to the sink, but she couldn't remove the smudges with the damp dish towel. "Lipstick. Honey, you have been up to some funny business. Maybe some lighter fluid. You got any lighter fluid?"

"Upstairs, I think," I told her.

"Well, come on before they come back in. Oliver Eugene, you hear me talking to you?"

In my room she dumped lighter fluid on the dish towel and began pressing into the cloth. "Stand still! What was somebody's lips doing all the way down here? Stand still, I say!"

The intimacy of the operation was not appreciated and I suggested I take off my jacket, but she shook her head. "I'm almost finished. Where were you, boy?"

It was remarkably dark, that inquiry, and I heard her heavy breathing. My suspicion was confirmed when she said, in a voice unfamiliar to me, "Sit down here and relax with old Della Mae," and as she said it I was given a gentle but well-calculated push backwards to the bed. "'Fraid of old Della Mae?"

"Don't be silly, Della? Why should I be afraid of you?"

"I bet you're afraid of Della Mae."

"For crying out loud." I sat there avoiding her left knee at my thigh.

"Della Mae's tired," she said.

"Stop that crazy 'Della Mae' stuff, Della. Good gravy."

Her demeanor soured quickly and she got out of her half-recline. "Della Mae is my name. I got a right to call myself by my name, don't I?"

One couldn't argue with her; it took enormous energy. "Suit yourself, suit yourself," I told her, and before I'd barely finished speaking, she was unbuttoning her maid's dress down the front, with her hazel eyes looking yellowish in the half-dark. And her lips were hanging open.

"What on earth are you doing?" I got up, my hands in a rage.

"Those were lipstick marks," she said by way of an answer, rolling down her stockings.

"So what if they were? Della? Della! Della, stop that! Stop undressing!"

"You been holding out on old Della Mae." Her slip was half over her head, and she said from beneath it, "Haven't you?"

"Della, stop undressing in my room. Stop it, I say! Suppose they come back? Della!"

"Lock the door, honey. Besides, they think you're over in Kalamazoo."

It was shameless the way she removed her intimate garments—with a snappy, vicious disdain for them—and sat on the edge of the bed nude, with only her little maid's hat on, smoking.

"I'm leaving, Della. Della, I'm leaving."

"You leaving me in here alone? Ha. Suppose they come looking for me here. That'd shake 'em. You dare leave me here?"

"You'll get fired, Della. They'll dismiss you on the spot!"

"Like this, sugar?" She laughed but it was too dark to see her gold tooth. "I'm leaving with Maurie in a couple of days anyway. Come here, boy. You a fraidycat?"

"Della, for crying out loud! For—" There were murmurs on the lawn, giggling, getting closer to the open window. There was the barking laughter of Mrs. Klein outside of the window, and I could see the tops of their heads in the light from the kitchen below, the three of them, with Peacock struggling ahead. "They're coming, Della!"

Her folly turned to panic and she grabbed her clothes but they were in a jigsaw jumble; and then as though her defiance had returned, she dropped the clothes at her feet. "Lock the door, kid."

It did seem logical, even in my frenzy. But it did not lock, and I knew it did not lock, and I fiddled with the door as though I thought it would somehow, miraculously. "Listen, this isn't a funny joke. You've got to get out. You've got to get out."

"Come here," she said, and like some huge black beast on my bed, she sat in the dark waiting for her prey.

My eyes scouted the room, as though it were not the most familiar room in the world, and I spied the closet. "Please go," I whispered as I heard the voices enter the house. And then I heard Mrs. Klein say from the foot of the stairs, "I wonder if Oliver's in yet." The sound of a foot, I thought mounting the stairs, set me in action, and I jumped into the closet and locked myself in.

Della gurgled in the dark, outside the closet, from my bed. There were slits at nose height through which I could look, but there wasn't much of a moon out and I could only see the orange glow of her cigarette end, rising, falling, brightening into yellow as she drew on it.

"Della," I whispered through the slits, "get the hell out of my room. This is dangerous."

"You come back with all that lipstick stuff on you to torment Della Mae like that? You been pulling the wool over my eyes all this time?"

The closet was hot and hangers jabbed my neck. I fell over my shoes. "It's from a lady. Della, that lipstick. It's not the way—"

"Glory, child, I should hope it would be from a lady. Now come on out here and be nice to Della Mae. I'll be leaving this old place soon, forever and forever. I'll be saying good-by forever."

"Good-by."

"Don't be smart."

"Leave!"

"I just might sleep here. All night. Just like this, Oliver, less you come out."

"Oh, for crying out loud. Why do you have to go get The Nasties with *me*? I thought you only got The Nasties over white men."

"You're white," she said, giggling.

"Don't be like that, Della."

"Well, you *try* to be white."

"I don't."

"You do."

"Oh, damn, Della."

"Well, what's all that longhair music business and them books written in French and them—"

"You're being stupid."

"And I say you're trying to be white. So there."

"Well, I'm not and you can't get The Nasties over me. So there. And so please put your clothes back on before somebody comes. I'm going to walk right out of here and be sensible and go downstairs. I'm going to leave you here."

"And if I yell after you? And if I come running down the stairway naked? Running after you? In front of them all? Sounds crazy? You don't think I could do it? Want to try me? Buck naked and barefoot?"

"You're bluffing."

"Want to try me? I'm leaving anyway, buster. Remember? Aw, come on, don't torture old Della Mae like this, honey. You've got to give in sooner—Hush!"

She was the one talking, the nude lecheress, but my heart froze too. Aunt Harry, either at the foot of the stairs—or coming up!—shouted: "Oliver? Oliver Eugene? You home yet?" There was a thud or two, but soon the sound faded in the direction of the living room.

We both were silent, long after the danger had passed. The insane comedy had a tinge of grist in it: we seemed, both of us, to have been playing out some grotesque pageantry of our lives; Della was there, nude to the world, exposed, vulnerable, and gluttonous; and I, dressed and harnessed, was locked in a dark closet.

At last I heard squeaks from the bed.

"You dressing?"

"No."

"Get the hell dressed."

"No."

"This is adolescent. I'm coming out. I'm getting out of here and I'm going to turn on the lights. I'm going to call everybody. I'm going to expose you."

"What have I got to lose? Go on. Your auntie has heart trouble real bad. You think she could stand it if her little precious—"

"I'm not precious!"

"Come out and show me you aren't precious, precious."

"Goddamnit, Della, will you stop seducing me? You're ugly. You're ugly as homemade sin."

"I'm not. I know I'm not. I know that much."

"All right, you aren't ugly, but I don't care for you. Now, get out."

"You cared for the Lipstick Lady. Who was she?"

"None of your business."

"Well, guess I'll have me another cigarette and wait for my little old chickadee to make up his mind."

"He's not going to take you, you know. I bet he's not going to take you. To Chicago, Della. I know. Now put that in your coffee and drink it."

"Maurie?"

"Monsieur LeFleur. *Oui*."

"You're lying."

"I am?"

"Oliver? Don't play that. Oliver?"

"Okay. Don't say I never told you."

"It's a trick. I know it's a trick."

"You do, do you?"

"Oliver? Oliver?"

"Put your clothes on and I'll tell you."

"If—if it's a trick, I'll kill you."

"You putting your clothes on?"

"Yes, damnit, give me time. What you think I am? Houdini?"

"You got them off pretty damned quick. It's hot in here. Hurry."

"Oh, shut up . . . you're tricking me, if you're . . . Oh, Oliver, you are kidding me, aren't you? Oliver?"

"Hurry, I'm burning up."

"Come on out if you're in such a hurry. I'm practically done up anyway."

She was putting on her stockings when I came out of the closet, wringing wet. "Now, what's this lie about Maurie not taking me to Chicago?"

"Keep your voice down, for crying out loud. It's no lie, at least I don't intend it as a lie. Della . . . Della, he's a crook. Pure and simple." I told her all about that night on the roof and I said, "You can't trust him. You just can't. He'll ditch everybody when he gets his loot. I really believe that, Della."

"Maurie? He won't ditch me. He won't ditch me."

"We'll see. You willing to bet?"

"You trying to put fear into me? You lying to me? He said he knew ways for me to have some furs and some clothes and he could set me up in Chicago. I take it with a grain of salt—the fur business and all, but he could get me started. Set up. He *promised*, Oliver. That dirty dog, he promised."

"When?"

"All along. All along he promised. He can't go back on his promise. He can't do that to me, because I can't stand being poor always, cooking and cleaning up after people for the rest of my life. And what am I going to do in this place? Oh, lord, what am I going to do in this town? Mrs. K kicks off one day and I get a two weeks' salary and I go to cook and clean for—for who? For some other white woman with lots of money. Jesus, no."

I sat on the bed near her, but in the dark I could only see the dull shine of the gold earring piercing her ear. "You could get married," I suggested.

"To what? A chauffeur? Chauffeur quality, that's me. The men in this town I could marry make no more money than I make. And I'm tired of it, tired of it, you hear me? I'm not about to waste away behind somebody's sink!"

The prospect was dreary, but then what else was there, really. "What would you do in Chicago? Specifically?"

She slapped her thigh in the dark. "What do you think? I've got only one thing. One thing, honey. God gave some people money and talent and the right color skin, but when He came around to Della Mae, well, Our Father Who Art in Heaven ran out of supplies. So I'm going to use what he did give me," she said, slapping her thighs again. "When I'm an old gray thing I can repent and pray and go to church and carry on with prayer meetings and all that, but now, now I'm going to get some goodies out of life, and if this is the way I've got to do it, then this is the way I've got to do it. . . . Damn Maurie, if he's lying to me . . . I don't put nothing past that bastard. But if he's lying to me—and I'll find out if he is—I'll just pick up and go to Chicago on my own. Honey, Della Mae is going to Chicago if it's the last thing she does. Oh, how long, how long, have that evenin' train been gone, Oliver? I'm going by hook or crook. With Maurie or alone. You hear me? Baby doll, there're going to be some changes made. You hear me?"

Bertram was putting the cow away and crickets began scratching their legs. We sat there on the bed listening to them a long time. What could I say? Della's way out seemed wrong, but the fact remained, it was a way out. I wished for her sake that Maurice LeFleur would leave with her, for I had an uneasy feeling that she knew less about the World Out There than she pretended; but I doubted that he had a taste for whoremongering.

Still, the thought of Della on windy streets, walking streets or beckoning from behind chintz curtains, made me ache.

"And you'll leave when?" I asked.

She took out a tissue from her pocket and folded it in half. I wondered if she'd begun to cry. "Saturday night after the séance—if he goes with me. If not—if not, I'll go. I'll go."

Bertram slammed the barn door and I heard footsteps downstairs. "You know I'd better go announce myself. It's way past dark and Aunt Harry is probably jittery thinking I'm still in Kalamazoo."

"What would you do if you was me, Oliver? Answer me that! Don't leave, Oliver, before you answer me that. Oliver, please don't just walk off and not answer, god-damnit, what *would* you do if you was me? Rot here? Can't I go to Chicago if I want to?"

I was standing at the door as she called after me, but I could not think of a bon mot to hand her; it was enough that I secretly kissed her from across the room in the dark.

"Oh, Oliver," she said, hoarsely. "If you was me . . . if you was me . . ." she began again as I left her in the room, the frightened glitter of the earring nibbling through her ear.

Downstairs it wasn't difficult to convince them that I'd come home before dark. In fact, they didn't seem to care; a minor crisis was in the air: Aunt Harry and Mrs. Klein were not speaking to each other. I had no idea when open hostilities began, but I'd seen for days their sly rivalries. They'd both gone through every piece of summer finery they possessed, with changes of dress for lunch, for tea, for dinner, in honor of the visiting thief.

LeFleur was reading an astrological magazine beneath a Tiffany lamp, and the ladies were playing solitaire in opposite corners of the room, pouting and wishing they were playing gin rummy with each other. From Mrs. Klein came a solicitous murmur (though she barely looked up from her cards) concerning my health: "You seem listless, dear, you feeling all right? You had your supper, I hope."

"Yes, thanks. I ate."

Aunt Harry, who was cheating with her cards, said, "You don't get enough exercise, if you ask me. Letting her make a white boy out of you is beginning to tell on your health."

I sat as far away from LeFleur as I could decently manage and diddled with my poem, trying to fit "sequestered destiny" and "playground in Eden" into an iambic meter.

There was silence in the room for a while, except for the sound of shuffling cards and the turning of LeFleur's astrological pages. Aunt Harry looked over at the canopy head beneath the Tiffany and said, startling us all, "Oliver, come over here a minute." I thought she wanted me to check her card game. "And bring your pencil. And that paper, too."

With complete disregard for my work-in-progress, she tore off paper (right under my last line—"Shetland ponies on a beach") and scribbled in her skinny writing: *Tell Mrs. Klein that Maurice LeFleur doesn't like avocados. We ought to have a nice simple green salad like I said we ought to.*

I raced this across the living room and put it on Mrs. Klein's card table, and she snatched the pencil from my hand. She wrote in big, childish letters: *Ask your Aunt who's running this household.*

Aunt Harry couldn't wait for me to reach the other side of the long room, but when she got the message she tore it up, accompanied with great noise, into a million pieces, and began humming a song without words, or much melody, to show just how unperturbed she was.

My job as courier was finished, so I sat down and faced my Shetland ponies on a beach.

"Mr. LeFleur," Mrs. Klein soon said, in bel canto, "if there's too much disturbance"—her glance shot across the room to Aunt Harry—"in this room for you, you may care to use the study." And then puffing a bit on her cigarette, she added, "I do apologize for the unruliness of my household."

Aunt Harry increased her volume—the tune was somewhere between "Abide with Me" and "Waltzing Matilda," but one couldn't be at all sure.

"Oh, no. No bother," Maurice LeFleur said, engrossed with warlockcraft. But his concentration had been disturbed and he looked at me. "Enjoy the movie, kid?"

I probably overdid my pretense of surprise as I looked up from my Shetland ponies on a beach and said, "Oh, yes, yes, very much," and lowered my head again to my task.

But that didn't discourage him. "What did you see?"

I started to produce any old title, but I noticed, just in time, the Kalamazoo *Gazette* at his feet. "God, I can't even remember the—"

"Oliver Eugene!" Aunt Harry shouted. "How many times have I told you not to use the Lord's name in vain?"

Mrs. Klein giggled. "Yes, dear. He will hold you guilty for using his name in vain." Her admonishment had a jazzy little bounce to it, which, unfortunately, did not escape Aunt Harry's quick ears.

"That boy is going to live up to Christian principles," Aunt Harry said, "even if he does read all those atheism books." She put her cards on the table. "I won't have him grow up a heathen."

Mrs. Klein smiled down at her six of clubs. "Oliver, tell your aunt," she said, absolutely giddy that *she'd* remembered they were not speaking, "that I'm not a Christian, thank God. I'm a Jew. I don't have all of her puritanical conflicts."

Aunt Harry began humming again. This time she was two registers too high, and there wasn't any melody to it whatsoever, but there was, except for the eerie lieder, peace for about ten minutes.

The next addition to the discordancies of the night was a rather vicious gurgle of rum in a glass. Mrs. Klein made a great production of taking off the top, pouring, and replacing the bottle on the window cupboard. She almost—but didn't quite—smacked her lips and said "Aaah." Almost. Aunt Harry, though, had the fortitude to resist comment.

"Oliver, dear," Mrs. Klein said conversationally, shuffling her cards, "you know that Mr. LeFleur is going to try the séance tomorrow night?"

"Tomorrow? Tomorrow's Friday. I thought Saturday."

Her little fat hands picked up her rum glass. She took a sip and shook her head. "No. Tomorrow. Isn't it exciting?"

"Very."

Aunt Harry made a sound that was not readily definable; it was not a grunt or a verbal comment, and it had come and gone so quickly it could not be intelligently analyzed. All of us looked at her, waiting for further illumination, but she was silent and bent her fiberglass hair over her aces and spades and diamonds and kings, quite aware we were all watching, waiting.

"Excuse me," I said, leaving the room. "I want a soda."

"There's only punch, dear," Mrs. Klein said, and with her arm stretched out into the middle of the air she waved me to attention. "Be a lambkin and bring me my cigarettes from the study, won't you?"

Fine. Now I had an excuse to go to the study, and I didn't waste a minute getting my call through to Kalamazoo. It was the butler, Lorenzo, who answered, thank God, and not Patricia Jo.

"Is Jerome Klein there, please?"

"Who is calling, please?"

"This is—I'm calling from Green Acorns. Is he there?"

"Just a moment, please."

There was a chance that he and Patricia Jo might be dining, that he wouldn't be able to—"Hello, Jerome? Oliver. I can't talk very much. We . . . No, nothing's wrong—yet. Nobody's sick. Now listen, can you meet me? Not here . . . I was at your place today . . . Yes . . . Maybe she forgot to tell you. It's important. It's about that fortune teller, Maurice LeFleur, the man they wanted to bring from Chicago . . . Right . . . Right . . . Well, he's here and he plans to do his thing tomorrow night. . . . Yes . . . Yes . . . Any time, I don't care. . . . Four? Four-thirty? Okay, say across from the Bijou . . . No, no, they won't let me in the bar, but if you're on time . . . let's say that dinette down from the Bijou. The one with the circus poster in the window. You'll see. It's air-conditioned. . . . All right . . . fine. Four sharp. Yeah, see you."

My hand was not yet off the phone when Maurice LeFleur opened the door. There in the dark room, with only the hall light seeping in behind him, I felt like a criminal. He stared at me and I could not move.

"She wondered what was taking you so long," he said, flipping on the light. "That might help, don't you think?"

His lock of inky hair sliding down his canopy head was wet and his vest was unbuttoned. He seemed very tired. Despondent, even.

A piece of sweat sat over his Picasso lips and in the corner of his mouth there was a toothpick. He found Mrs. Klein's cigarettes on the desk by the door, and still looking at me, his rabbit eyes on me, he snapped off the lights. He closed the door. He left me in the dark.

3

Belle Thompson had a catharsis about every other month, or so she use to tell me when I read to her the Shakespeare sonnets. I wondered, as I passed her house on the way to town, when she'd had her last one; I had not read in the papers of a funeral or wedding in Allegan for quite some time. In times of draught, presumably, she improvised.

As I walked down the dirt road that came at one point near her vined and ivy-smothered cottage I noticed that all her shades were drawn, but the radio was on, which meant that somebody was around. She, or perhaps her roué brothers. But I'd passed Belle Thompson's place a dozen times since my sonnet-reading days and would have gone on today had it not been for the sound of familiar male laughter. Nobody else in the world was cursed with laughter like that (a kind of Hail, Hail, the Gang's All Here intrusion on the senses) except Jerome. My watch said ten to three, so I supposed he'd decided to kill time with Belle. That was his business. Yet the thought of the long hike to town under the blue-hot sky wasn't a pleasant thought—especially when Jerome's big fat black air-conditioned limousine was standing idle by Belle's shrubs.

Belle herself saved me the trouble of deciding how I could most gracefully intrude upon the afternoon tryst. She came skittering, on high plastic heels, into view as she crossed the patio with two tall frosted glasses decked with cherries. She stopped dead in her plastic-heeled tracks and pushed her sunglasses gently down her nose with a crook of her wrist. She blinked a bit, to believe her eyes, and said, "Hi, honeybunch!"

Belle was known as a Plump Widow; she'd been a widow forever and she'd been plump forever, and she had little inclination to change either status. She was a Renoir woman. Her limbs were full-fleshed; however, they were called luscious by her friends (male) and elephantine by her enemies (female). Quite often she was motivated to take odalisque attitudes, i.e., she usually was in a position of recline on one or the other of her hips. During those weeks of reading sonnets (until Mrs. Klein and Aunt Harry put a stop to it) I rarely saw her walk or sit upright. Her world was the divan, the settee, the hammock, the couch. In fact, there was not a single upright chair in her entire cottage. Yet there was not a sickly aura about her reclining positions; there were always bits of frenzy surrounding her chaise longue, her bed, for her hands did a thousand things (fanning, picking chocolates); her hands were as gay as bees always. It was only her face I objected to—an attractive face, more or less, but the contours in it were unsteady. Her hair, though, was thrilling: it was frizzled Colette hair, wild and uncertain, and its color range included apricot, russet, kumquat, strawberry, ocher, peach, or, alas, just plain old brown when she couldn't get to the beauty salon or when she was hot on the trail of a catharsis.

Mrs. Klein said she was a whore. Her friends in the town said she was a paramour. Aunt Harry said she was a woman who had fallen on evil ways. Benson once said she had *joie de vivre.* And as I say, I only know her from the days of the sonnets and her foot infection. She lay there those days, when I read to her, fanning her ocher hair with a Japanese fan, and the flash from her ruby rings got in my eyes. Although she would say, rather low and from one side of her mouth, "Aw, read them sonnets, honeybunch, read 'em," she would at the same time take sips of Cherry Heering and then fidget with the radio to get the top ten songs on *Afternoon Music Patrol.* Sometimes, with a mouth filled with a bon bon, she would ask me to repeat a line or two and would interrupt me in the middle of it, as though she were wrestling with Ecstacy, and murmur: "Aw, read it, honey, read that thing! Read it in the name!" Exclamations of this sort were accompanied, invariably, with gestures best not described. Sometimes, so that I could watch her carefully as she did her nails, I would pretend to read one of the two sonnets I knew by heart— *How like a winter hath my absence been . . .* or *Not marble, nor the gilded monuments . . .* Her eyes were darker blue than Mrs. Klein's and she blinked a great deal.

She was blinking now from the glare of the Allegan sun. She had a ribbon in her hair.

"Come hither sweet stranger," she said in an Elizabethan giggle. "Haven't seen you in a coon's age." Her remark startled her, and to offset her tinge of regret she clip-clopped across the stone patio to stick a red kiss upon my cheek. She was there making the oily imprint on me, with highball glasses in each hand extended skywards, as Jerome came out to the edge of the patio. Through a peek-hole in her Colette hair (burnt orange today), I saw Jerome's beefy shoulders hunch up as he mouthed: "Jesus H. Christ."

"Well, come on over, honeybunch," Belle said. "Got time for a quickie? I'm in swoon-haste to get into town."

It didn't seem prudential to acquiesce to any sort of "quickie" at Belle Thompson's until one knew just what she had in mind. In this case it was a Tom Collins, which Jerome began making with passionate energy.

"You do want a drink?" he said, and sounded quite drunk.

"Yes, please. I do. Uh, actually—actually, I was walking into town to see you."

"Yeah. I was on my way to see you, too. Stopped. Stopped for a quick little drink."

"Yeah, well, this was on my way to town—you see, I always cut across this way to go through the cemetery, and Belle, she called and . . ."

Belle stopped drinking and looked right and left. "My, my, my. Methinks there's nervous tension." Her lips twitched. "Now where in the hell are my beads? Now that Jock and Eddie are here . . ." She was on her hands and knees looking under the patio couch. "Now that those two are here, I can't find a damn thing. Everything was disorganized in the right way before, but now everything is *disorganized* disorganized," and she added, saying it from the side of her mouth and as low as she could manage for midday, "if you get what I mean." Then, more to Jerome than to me, she said, "Drink, drink up. I'll go give the kitchen one more search."

We were alone and Jerome spoke immediately. He said, "Belle's brothers left her car in town. They went into Detroit last night by train. She's going after her car."

"Oh, yes," I said fatuously, and before I could stop it, I tacked on, "I used to read to Belle when she had that foot trouble." I was steadily making it worse; "that foot trouble" assumed he had prior and perhaps even intimate knowledge about Belle Thompson, and this very assumption ensconced as it was in "that foot trouble" implied that I, too, knew Belle prior to this encounter, and perhaps more than casually. Or maybe this was splitting hairs. Jerome chewed on the end of his cigar and Belle yelled from the disorganized innards of her cottage: "Glory be, kiddies! La Belle found 'em! The rascals were in the freezer!"

The rascals turned out to be beads of large transparent stones, faintly streaked with lavender. She gave us a quickie fashion show and picked up her drink. "Don't know how they got in the freezer. I *never* put them *there*. But they are heavenly. Cold this way, I mean."

For about two ridiculous minutes we all drank the tall drinks without saying a word. "Listen," Belle said, picking out the cherries in her drink, "I know you two have some talk for each other—and there isn't any point of you carting me to town, Jerome. If you want, you—"

"Don't be foolish, Belle. In this hot sun you going to walk?"

She peeked in her compact to see if everything was all right around her face. "To be honest, it's not the sun that worries me—it's these shoes. I'd never make it in these shoes. Tell you what, drive me over to Irenie's and— No, no, I mean it. Me and Irenie can go on to town from her house. I haven't gassed with her in a co—in ages."

"But, Belle, the car is sitting right—"

"Oh, stop it, you big old chivalrous thing you, and do as I say. It's no time at all to town from Irenie's and besides you can have your summit meeting right here." She picked up her purse with the little yellow sequins on it and patted my cheek. "And anyways, honeybunch might want a little refreshment. You know bloody well at his age he can't get liquor in town."

Jerome had no choice and headed towards the driveway. "I'll wait here," I told him, realizing what an unnecessary statement that was inasmuch as they both were practically already in the car.

"Adieu, honeybunch," Belle said, sticking on her smudged sunglasses. "Adieu."

Jerome looked very hot and bothered. He pulled the limousine up under a shaded patch on the drive and came up to the patio.

"Belle's odd," he said right away, and made a big whiskey with one cube of ice in it.

"Yes, she is."

"A good woman, though."

"Yes, she is."

"I mean underneath everything."

"Yes, she—"

"Good Christ, Oliver, can't you say anything else but 'yes, she is, yes, she is'? Good Christ!" He turned and found a seat. "Sorry. I'm jumpy. This goddamned heat."

"It is a hot day," I said, wishing fervently I could stop responding so inanely, could end my uneasiness. I had always been able to handle Jerome in the milieu of Green Acorns, but away, here, I found no smugness to protect me. I looked for all the telltale signs of his coarseness—his bad taste in clothing; the unlit cigar, which whenever removed from his mouth, was muddy and obscene; the cluster of red veins, like Rorschach patterns, sticking out on his cheeks; his beefy, bullish shoulders that were often damp with sweat beneath his jacket, even in wintertime—they were all there, those telltale signs, but they no longer left within me a feeling of—what? Security had it been? I had always fed upon his coarseness so that I might all the more appreciate my sensibilities, so that I might bask in the glow of my self-discoveries. There on the patio it came as a jolt, the recognition of my malaise, my neurotic urge; and the recognition I would not have acknowledged at all had I not tried once again to seek a feeling of smugness from those traits and signs I thought coarse, that I pronounced inferior. What was it? Why would it not work again for me? Certainly the success of my little neurotic game was not contingent upon a geography and a milieu, though I pondered this awhile, thinking it might be the answer; I had not, after all, seen Jerome outside Green Acorns, away from the ladies. A couple of occasions, perhaps. But not alone. Alone with Jerome. And here at Belle's, watching him get tighter and tighter in the afternoon heat, I felt that I did not know him at all.

He finally took off his jacket—yes, sweaty shoulders, and there were deep wet rings under his armpits, in antic symmetry.

"Yes, Belle's a damn good person underneath it all."

I couldn't force myself into a bright mood for the life of me; I thought, for instance: Belle is a good woman underneath what? Her clothes? But somehow, though it was the kind of obvious corn Jerome appreciated, I couldn't bring myself to say it, and, too, I wasn't sure how much I could joke around about the merry pranks of La Belle Thompson. In lieu of a Thompson anecdote I said, feeling lightheaded from the drink (fortified generously while they were away), "Maurice LeFleur is giving his séance at midnight."

"Yeah."

"Midnight tonight."

"So you said on the phone."

"And he's after jewels. It's obvious, isn't it?"

"Yeah, yeah."

"You hear me, Jerome? That necklace of Mrs. Klein's."

Jerome drank two or three big bear swallows of pure whiskey, and then he raised his eyebrows and threw out a hand in a beefy burlesque of cynicism. "With your aunt there? With Aunt Harry? He should live so long."

"She's got the LeFleur bug too. Moreover, I didn't even mention it to her."

He pretended to explode, but he was getting too drunk to be effective. "What? You on his side or theirs? Now listen, you know I half expect you to watch over things. *Some*body's got to keep an eye open at that place. The least you could—"

"I'm not a watchdog, for crying out loud! Isn't it enough for me to tell you? *You* were the one so much against it. *You* forbid it. *You* said you didn't want a charlatan running loose around the place. Now you're all—well, you act as though you don't care. If *you* don't care, God, *I* don't."

I'd raised my voice at him for the first time in my life and he seemed as stunned over it as I. After a bit he leaned back in the wrought iron chair and scratched his hairy stomach beneath his shirt. "That was before Patricia Jo—" He tried a confidential laugh and said, "Listen, old bean, I haven't been honest with you. Now, man to man. I'm being honest. Patricia Jo told me the whole goddamn thing."

"Well, then why—"

"Not until after you called last night. You know how it goes when you take up bed and board with a bitch. It was like this, see. You called. She wanted to know. I wouldn't say. Then she had one of her tantrums—and she can be a shrew, my old lady can. Then I said it was you. Then she told me about your trip over to our house. And she up and decided she wanted to come over for the occasion tonight. So you see, old bean, that's just about how the cookie crumbled."

Although I'd nearly begged Patricia Jo to tell him, I now felt betrayed. "So what are you going to do about it?"

"Nothing."

"*Nothing?* But you've got to do something. You just can't . . . can't. Oh, I wash my hands right here and now. Nobody cares so why should I care? How did I start this one-man mission to stop LeFleur? God. Aunt Harry wants it, Mrs. Klein wants it, Patricia Jo wants it, Maurice LeFleur wants it, now *you* want it. What is this? How'd I get snarled up into this mess to begin with? Huh, Jerome?"

Jerome laughed and pulled the whiskey bottle closer. "Ah, what the hell. Let 'em have a bit of fun raising spooks from the dead and all that. What the hell. If they want it . . . old bean, you know, you're the one who doesn't want it, looks like to me."

I felt muscles in my neck jumping but I told him right off the bat, "*Me?* Want that séance? I couldn't care less. It's got nothing to do with me. I don't care if they have one every night. It's got nothing to do with me. If they want to see Sargeant or hear him talk, or whatever, that's their business. I don't know Sargeant. Don't want to know Sargeant. Couldn't care less about Sargeant. That's a fact. You don't believe me? I'm going to make a little more for me to drink. All right?"

He looked up, his eyelids heavy, and drank all the whiskey in his glass. "Be careful with that stuff, buddy old buddy, or you'll end up like Mark." He poured himself more whiskey, without water, without ice, and said, "He's a drunk, you know. Like his old dad."

"You bragging about that, Jerome?"

He didn't answer because he was staggering towards the lilacs, looking aquamarine. "For crying out loud, Jerome, are you drunk? How long have you been at it?"

This he couldn't answer either, for his curly red head was leaning out into the sun, at the edge of the patio, being sick all over the lilacs. The noise he made was more objectionable than the pale pink-brown spewing, but it was the bitter end when he grabbed his glass of whiskey to rinse his mouth, spraying that whiskey mouthwash, glistening gold, over the lilacs into the sunlight. Then he sat down and commenced swilling again, ignoring patches of vomit on the front of his shirt.

"Are you crazy, Jerome? You're getting stoned," I told him, and I'm afraid indignantly, as though he had no right to get drunk. "How long have you been at the bottle?"

"All my life—since early this morning if you want to know," he said, his words sliding along together, hooked together like a choo-choo train.

The heat began to agitate the stench Jerome had caused by vomiting. I was forced to go inside for a mop and pail. I had not taken the mop out of the hot water before I found it sailing about my feet, rolling across the floor. He had kicked it with drunken, beefy power, and he shouted loud enough to be heard in town: "You goddamn priss-foot! What in the hell are you doing? Haven't you seen puke before?"

It seemed perfectly clear what I was doing and I could not accept his drunkenness as an excuse for his vicious behavior. I was about to tell him so, too, but the brief and violent activity proved too much for him: he fell forward, to his knees, then to his face, on the stones of the patio. He lay there in squalor and bliss.

My first inclination was to leave, to go home, but flies gathered around the soiled stones and streaks of sudsy water were everywhere. This time I was able to clean without interference, and I mopped quietly around his body sprawled face down on the stones. When I finished, in my own good time, I shook him, tentatively at first, and then with increased violence until he gave a bit of a stir. "Get up, Jerome, for crying out loud. You want Belle to find you like this? Get up!" He merely flopped an arm on the stone floor with a lazy impatience. Partly because flies were gathering around him (fat ones with green-blue sheens on their wings), and partly out of retaliation, I decided to take upon myself a task that would irritate him, though I knew it probably would involve quite a struggle for me. I pulled him over on his back and undressed him to his underclothes (boxer shorts with red pitchforks and red devils stamped on them), and went in to clear a path to Belle's shower, i.e., removal of books, a hot water bottle, candy boxes, a purple kimono, a shoe tree, and three ginger ale bottles. (When I returned, a thick green fly was sitting on Jerome's lip, inspecting, wringing its hands, as though it were expressing appreciation for the summer at its height.) Then, rather like lugging some hairy beast through a forest, I lugged Jerome (pulled him by his armpits) across Belle's patio, into her house, into the shower room floor, and I did not care in the least if I bumped or scarred him along the way. He murmured and moaned but seemed in general not to be very concerned about his fate, though the icy water that pounded on his body caused him at first considerable alarm. "Sargeant! Sargeant! Hey! Hey! What ya doing?"

His eyes were wide open and he was calling me Sargeant. "It's Oliver, Jerome, and you're drunk."

"Drunk? Drunk?" The cold water pounding upon his head turned his hair to red ringlets: he looked for a minute like Julius Caesar. Then with his eyes closed he tried to raise himself from his dumped-on-the-floor sitting position, but the effort was not worth it, so he sat there staring, with lazy eyes, out from the streaming water. "Got to get to the séance. Got to get . . . Sargeant, you going to be at the—"

"Snap out of it, Jerome. Come on."

"Sargeant?"

"It's Oliver."

"Yeah. You not Sargeant. You not. Bring a drinkie, huh? A little old pretty gold drinkie?" He stood up, nearly revived by the thought of a drink. "I like a drinkie. Mama likes a drinkie. Mark likes a drinkie. Gemme drinkie. Be a good *goy* and gemme little drinkie."

For a bit I thought he would fall asleep on his feet; his head dropped to his chest and his hands fell palm outwards from his thighs. Then suddenly he hit up at the pouring water as though he thought it would go away. "Stop, stop them, Sargeant. Stop the water, Sargeant."

"Hey, I'm getting pretty tired of this Sargeant business. You feeling sober yet?"

"Sorry, old beanie weanie. I like you, hate him, like you . . . killed himself, killed himself, killed himself." He chanted, beating his buttocks (the red devil shorts had slid to his knees) and stamping his feet as though he were a galloping horse.

"Wait, wait. Let me turn off the water. You're making a mess."

And as soon as I turned off the water, he fell forward, icy and wet, into my arms, knocking me with his two hundred pounds into the sink. For quite a time I could not free myself—half falling, pressed into the edge of the sink with Jerome's dead weight flopped over me. Moreover my elbow had mashed yards of toothpaste over the bathroom and Jerome's dangling hand knocked a shampoo bottle to the floor, where it smashed into a hundred thousand pieces. To the right I was afraid I'd slip on toothpaste; to the left I was afraid I'd cut Jerome's feet. For some time I was trapped there, the edge of the sink pressing into the small of my back and Jerome's dead pounds on top of me, nude as a store dummy model. His nose was somewhere near my collar bone, for I felt his hot snores reminding me there that he was not dead, that he was simply a two-hundred-pound weakling, that my back was to the wall (i.e., sink), and that I was faced with the problem of his nudity. Eventually I could cover his body, but I wondered how I would manage to forget the brief and naked exposure of his mind.

The first step was to get him back into the shower area, which I did fairly painlessly, though I fear I bumped his head as I lowered him. Then—it seemed hours (and Jerome snored naked in the shower)—I swept and mopped and double mopped up the glass from the shampoo bottle. I even let the floor dry before I pulled him out, by the shoulders, and I left him on his back to dry. Why I bothered to tidy up Jerome's mess, I can't imagine; Belle could not possibly tell where her havoc stopped and someone else's started. She did, however, notice the one thing I'd overlooked; as soon as she got out of her car she screamed: "*Merde!* What bastard puked on my lilacs? *Who* puked on my lilacs?" I heard her heels tapping cross the patio. "Jerome, you fool! You let that boy get drunk? Jerome?" She took off her sunglasses to see me. "Honeybunch!"

"Jerome," I said, pointing to his nude body on her Bergundy rug, "passed out."

"Oh, the dear old silly thing," she said, bending over his body, but when she straightened up she giggled. "He looks like a big hunk of salmon, doesn't he? Well, put a shroud over the body, darling, and I'll make coffee."

I couldn't find his red-devil-and-pitchfork shorts, so I dismissed that item, wiggled the rest of his clothes on him, and waited for Belle to bring the coffee. As it turned out, we drank the coffee and let Jerome sleep, for he seemed happy enough, sleeping there at our feet.

"Poor old toughie," Belle said over her cup. "I knew he was afraid of meeting you today, but heavens, not this afraid. You know, he's always held his liquor before."

"Afraid? *He* was afraid of meeting me?"

"Ah, yes, I guess. He told me about this parlor game you folks are having down there tonight. Poor old thing felt duty bound to stop it, but he wanted it like the dickens." She looked over at me and turned her chin sideways. "Says you've got some kind of bug to stop the fun. That true, honeybunch?"

"*He* was dead against it. *He* was. At first. The henpecked—"

"What's it matter?" she said, slapping her hand at the air. (She could dismiss tuberculosis, principalities, income tax, and Freudian complexes with her hand that way when she wanted to.) "Listen, looks like Jerome-baby's going to be out for a spell. Why don't you pour some more coffee," she said, trotting away into the depths of her cottage. When she came out she was done up in a white silk kimono. Just like the movies: she'd slipped into something loose. And when she slid, right hip first, on the chaise longue, I could not help but think that it was all preparatory for seduction. And, too, over and over in my mind I heard Della's taunt: you a fraidycat, you a fraidycat. I guess because the weather was so hot and I'd had so much to drink and Belle lay on her hip the way she did, I said, with Jerome sleeping at my feet, "You think I'm too young?"

Her odalisque hip moved in a jerk and she smoothed out her white silk kimono with the hand bedecked with her ruby ring. "One is never too young. One is always too old, but never too young." She was talking quickly, almost like a sports announcer at a prize fight. "You'll make a brilliant career at college, I'm sure of that. You may be younger than most, but look, right in town, right now, everybody is talking about your *cum laudes* and all, and nobody in your graduating class can hold a candle to—"

"No, I don't mean—I mean, I was—"

"Don't say it." She sat up in an upright position and drank down all of her coffee. "It's better you don't say it."

"You *know* what I want to say?"

"I think I know what you want to say, and if you want to say what I think you want to say I think you better not say it. You'd be better off speaking to me low of Baudelaire. Or would you like to play scrabble?" She got up to get the game. "Wouldn't you?"

"No. You know I don't like that game and you ought to tell me why." And she should! Every single encounter in the past had given me the impression—

"Oh, honeybunch, don't get all upset and sore. It's . . ."

"I'm too young."

"No." Some of her old self came back for a minute; she had been, for the last few moments, rattled and not the least bit self-assured. "Youngness," she said, hardly moving her lips, "has got nothing to do with it." She pressed her empty cup to her bosom and looked helter-skelter about corners of her room as she spoke. "I've—I've bestowed favors—" Her archaic phrase seemed not to embarrass her as she paused; she seemed puzzled, as though she couldn't quite remember where it was from. The Elizabethans? Charlotte Brontë? Descartes? "I've bestowed favors on—on a couple of men who were young, though I don't make a practice of it. I do use some restraint, and that is—"

"Because of Jerome, then?"

She leaned forward, poked Jerome with her black satin slipper, and assumed a frank attitude. She wasn't being frank at all. "Honeybunch, I'd just as soon not go into it. Why don't you go out and get yourself—" She stopped, and leaning back she said, "What brings on all this sudden passion anyway? The summer heat?"

"I knew it. I knew it. It's because of Jerome, then." I stood up, irritated, but pleased to some extent that I'd been aggressive, even if the result had not been successful. At least I wasn't a "fraidycat."

Belle Thompson slapped her hands together as if she were chasing geese or calling children back to class. This gesture seemed far too homey for her and I stared, I guess, with my mouth open. "Sit back down. If there's one thing I can't stand it's wrong notions. Now you sit down, honey-bunch, and get this straight."

Her voice had hardened and she kept running her fingers through her burnt orange hair. A mean shot ran through me: How could I have entertained the idea with such a person in the first place?

"Now, listen," she said, "Jerome Klein doesn't own me. He doesn't keep me. He's got nothing to do with my decisions. He's got nothing to do with this—and you can tell him that, too, when he wakes up." She leaned forward, adjusting her kimono, and changed her voice back to a softer tone. "Sugar, it's not that you're not interesting. You're tall and you don't look sixteen or seventeen, and I like the way you move and you've got big hands and all that, and—well, actually, honeybunch, it's me. Me. It's just me. I've never bestowed any favors on a colored man—boy before."

My choice of action was to laugh or to storm about, but I was too stunned. This reason was outside of the realm. Della, raucous Della, had always proclaimed me white, and though I knew better, I never thought of being any color, or rarely, and now that she had put it this way, given this reason, placed this obstacle in front of what I deemed an easy seduction, I felt not pain or dismay but a curious loss. Loss of what? Moreover I could not fully comprehend; her reason seemed like one of Benson's theorems: it did not seem to fit, it did not seem to apply to the situation at all. Of course there had been things in the past. I was not from another planet; I read newspapers; I skirted around tricky situations at school dances, in the drama club. I was not, however, conditioned for the possibility of her refusal, the reasons for her refusal. It seemed so abstract. It seemed so theoretical. My breath was short in coming and I stood there with my arms dangling.

Belle tightened her kimono and frowned as though she were very concerned. "It's not that I'm prejudiced or anything, God knows. I'm really not. I don't have a prejudiced bone in my body. Neither does Eddie. Neither does Jock. Why, when I spent my two years at Western, I *roomed* with a colored girl. And don't you dare go figuring how many years back that was. And we were *that* thick." She demonstrated, with two of her ringed fingers. "It's just that I never have bestowed any favors on a colored man—boy before. I mean, it's just something one doesn't—can't—can't jump right into, honeybunch. I mean, you aren't mad at me or sore or anything, are you?"

I got my voice back and scraped together as much dignity as I could manage. "I beg your pardon for the effrontery. You must understand that—that I thought there was a certain amount of provocation—on your part. Each time I've come up here—"

She giggled and threw back her kimonoed arms. For her, the crisis was over and her juices were again flowing in the fashion necessary to promulgate her *joie de vivre*. "Yes, yes, La Belle has been a bit naughty, hasn't she? I'm a natural-born seductress, honeybunch. That's why I could see what was in your eyes right off. I'm afraid wickedness runs through my bones, but I don't mean it half the time. Maybe I teased you a bit, but I didn't mean it. I—"

"You were just keeping in practice then? For your serious encounters, huh?"

Belle flapped the air in front of her hand. "Touché, touché, honeybunch, you *can* laugh, after all. Now let's stop this will-I-won't-I fuss, because I won't—at least not until I get used to the idea. Now," she said, taking my cup, "now that we've gotten our urges all sorted out and tucked back in place, let's try to wake Jerome-baby up. All right?"

Jerome lay face down with his two hands tucked, like soft mittens, under his nude throat.

"Come on Jerome-baby," she said, slapping his face much harder than she realized. "Wake up, boy. Wake up for mamakins." She got another good slap in, which was almost powerful enough to bring back the dead. "Come on, thataboy, thataboy."

When Jerome was in half decent shape it was seven-thirty, and by the time we said good-by to Belle it was eight o'clock. He was silent during the short drive down to Green

Acorns and only spoke when we saw Patricia Jo's tiny red Fiat near Bertram's wheelbarrow.

"She wanted to be here," he said, nothing more.

"For crying out loud, you arranged all this, didn't you? You two planned on being here. You . . ." I was too angry to go on. It was infuriating the way two perfectly twentieth-century people were making preparations to go along with LeFleur's pranks. Apparently they believed in magic a little bit; it was either that, or their desperation was so great they would play any game, with any rules, no matter how unreal, how bizarre. The betrayal choked me and it put me in a rage.

"So you believe something's going to happen tonight. Huh, Jerome?"

"Will you shut up?" We walked up to the house, and he said, "What are you afraid of?"

I was not afraid. I was not afraid. I was not.

4

The pre-séance dinner lacked gala and was excessively intense. Patricia Jo couldn't stop staring at Maurice LeFleur; she turned every two seconds as though to make sure he was not some exotic bird that might fly away, and he preened, as though he thought he heard us saying *Gloria in Excelsis LeFleur*, raising in silent little toasts his glass of Bordeaux. Jerome was fairly quiet, though he had every reason to be, and contributed to the proceedings only when his opinion was solicited. When it came time for coffee, we moved to the living room, which irritated Della considerably: it was a lot of putting on airs, she complained; the coffee was as good at the table—where it wouldn't spill on things—as it was in the living room. (This was aimed at Mrs. Klein, for she had a tendency to knock over coffee and tea cups, though, it must be admitted, she rarely wasted rum.) Besides, it was extra footwork, Della felt. "They just seen somebody do that in an English movie somewhere. I bet you anything."

Aunt Harry was remarkably polite. This meant, of course, that she was nervous. She never played upon her drums when she was nervous or frightened, and she hid her fear behind syrupy formalities. A high starched collar rose from her black lace dress, a dress I knew for a fact to be her very best, and every fiber of her fiberglass hair had been carefully brushed into place. Her eyes sparkled in their patchwork of wrinkles and her hands lay in her lap.

Patricia Jo wore black, too; this evening was going to be a State Occasion. She wore one strand of pearls about her neck and a thin line of mascara around her eyes. Off and on she'd turn pages in a magazine, and she tried desperately to make Light Conversation, but it was a failure, that; it was perfectly obvious to everyone that she couldn't keep her eyes focused on things and people in the room: Maurice LeFleur had gone upstairs to rest for an hour before he would come down to perform. I can't imagine what she expected—that perhaps he would spring down the staircase in swirling robes, beating a gong and saying hocus-pocus words? Or did she fear he would disappear? Well, the Teardrop was safe. Aunt Harry, somewhere in the bottom of her soul, had a deep stain of skepticism; Mrs. Klein's jewel was locked in its case and tucked in the wall hole behind the "Moose at Bay" picture at the top of the stairs.

Mrs. Klein had herself a rum on the rocks and said as little to Patricia Jo as she could without jeopardizing the temporary truce. Her hair looked very suspiciously blue-tinged, and she, too, wore her best summer dress—a peach color organdy with large black buttons on it. After several not very sincere attempts to find out why Jerome looked so peaked, she gave up and went back to her cigarettes.

We sat there—the three Kleins, Aunt Harry, and I—for many, many minutes. We seemed strangers waiting in a

station to take a train to another city. We were waiting
by pools of light from the Tiffany lamps, which hit the
floor at the edge of the sofa near Patricia Jo's feet and at
the bookcase near the bay window. We sat there, and for a
good while nobody moved. From deep within the back of
the house came Della's voice: "How long, how long, have
that evenin' train been gone . . ." It was barely audible, less
so than the sound of the clock, but the pain of it could
reach the heart.

"Excuse me," I said.

Aunt Harry perked up. "Where you going?"

"I'll be back, I'll be back," I said and headed for Della's
room. She was packing. "What are you doing?"

"Whatsit look like I'm doing, sonny boy?"

"You packing?"

Two suitcases were open on her bed and she was dressed
in slacks. "I told you I was getting out of here, and I'm
getting out of here."

"Alone then?"

"No," she said, looking at me for the first time. "I'm
going on to that motel down near the highway. Maurie's
going to meet me there."

"He said that, huh?"

"Yes, he said that. Now stop trying to put fear in my
heart, you hear?" The room was heavy with Turkish Kiss
Kologne and hangers fell from her closet to the floor. "I
can't wait to be gone. Can't wait. Say, you can do Della
Mae a tiny favor. I'm leaving this here note," she said, tapping a white envelope. "It's for your auntie to send me my
money when I get set up. You can give it to her, okay? I've
got some pay coming yet."

I took the note and we sat on the bed listening to crickets for a while. "He'll be a flop, won't he Della?"

"Maurie? Probably."

"What do you think'll happen?"

"Your auntie will make a scene. Throw things. Good Jesus, that woman can be evil when she wants to. Mark my word—she'll throw things. I don't suppose you can lend me some cash, can you?"

"Lend?"

"I didn't think so."

"Your partner in crime will have enough."

"You kidding?"

"He'll get some kind of fee, I'm sure."

"You're out of your mind with happiness about it, aren't you? Because he'll be a flop, I mean."

"Ecstatically."

"Oliver, something might happen to me."

"What?"

"It's not nice to be without money."

"You'll make out, Della, just be sincere."

"I can do without your sarcastic talk, I can tell you that."

I lit a cigarette to cut the aroma of her Turkish Kiss Kologne. "Don't you have any money? Anything?"

"Twelve dollars and thirty-seven cents. How long will that last?" She got up to finish packing, at the same hasty pace, as though she hadn't been interrupted. "And there won't be a lot coming in like I thought, I bet. The sonofabitch can't even find the—"

She stopped and glanced at me quickly with her eyes sharp hazel.

"The necklace he can't find, can he, Della?"

"Lord no, the goddamn thing is locked up somewhere. Gone."

"You've investigated?"

"I've noticed." She looked around the room once again. "That's it, honey. It's a wreck this room and the sink's full of dirty dishes, but tough titty, Della Mae is on her way. On her way!"

Although there was plenty of dash to her movements in the pair of gray slacks, her hands trembled as she snapped the locks shut on her suitcases. "You want to help me take them out? I'm going through the grove."

"What can I say? No? Come on."

For some reason I was rewarded in the backyard with a kiss on the forehead, a kiss that was shockingly platonic considering the source. "I still think you're a fool, Della. Do you even know *how* to get to the highway from here?"

She laughed hoarsely and a bit as though she would cry. "Brother, do I know how! I've been practicing in my mind for days. I go kitty-kat through the grove"—the north grove was black and moonlight never penetrated it—"then I walk for a good piece, and then I can see the car lights on the highway." Her mouth was shaking under the shadow of the tree. "Listen to that sound. Listen to them tires on the highway beating lickety-split to Chicago. Isn't that a lonesome sound?"

We were listening to the big trucks neck-breaking it down the highway but we both were watching the shadow of Maurice LeFleur behind his shade upstairs, pacing back and forth, back and forth, on the carpet. "That sonofabitch better meet me," she said, picking up her bags and running towards the black grove. She looked back once and I caught the gleam of her earring, just before she disappeared into the cluster of trees.

"Watch out for the dung," I shouted after her. "Don't step in the cow dung," I said, surprised to find my eyes filled with tears.

I came back into the house and found the pantry door half open. I could not see, but I heard voices: they were fussing at each other:

Aunt Harry whispered, "It's disgraceful for a woman of your age, Etta."

"You're no spring chicken yourself, Harriet. Now give me that bottle."

"No."

"Now stop it. This is *my* house and *my* rum and—"

"You're a regular rum head, that's what you are."

"Foot, I haven't had all that much today."

"Three bottles."

"Three bottles, three bottles. You're lying in your teeth. Or growing feeble-minded. Or both."

"Could as well be three or three dozen. Everywhere you turn there's a bottle. Just yesterday, as a matter of fact, Della brought out a bottle from your bedroom."

"It was only *one* little old bottle, for goodness' sake. And it was empty."

"Of course it was empty. You can't stand a bottle to stay full. Hurts you through and through to see a full bottle, I'll wager."

"Oh, hush, Harriet."

"A whole case of this stuff is under your bed right now, I'll wager."

"I'll wager *you* if you don't hand me that bottle, Harriet Gibbs!"

"But, Etta . . . tonight? Must you tonight? Mr. LeFleur . . ."

"Yes. Yes, I must. I need strength."

"Drink milk."

"Harriet Gibbs!"

As I left there was a spat. Somebody had spatted somebody with her hand. Nine to one it was Aunt Harry: she had a bad habit of going around spatting people with her long skinny hand.

LeFleur was still pacing back and forth on the carpet in his room, quite likely getting together spiritualistic energy, but I knocked on the door anyway and walked in before he could reply. "Listen," I told him right off, "if you don't meet Della over at that motel, you really will be a rotten bastard."

He was standing by the window in his shirt sleeves and fingering the chain at his vest. His tongue rolled over his lips and he seemed to be trying to work up a smile.

"I know you're a crook. And a fake. And—and worse. But what about Della?"

"Tsk, tsk," he clicked, pressing his inky lock to his forehead. "You've got some mighty harsh words for me this evening, haven't you?"

"Cut the bullshit, LeFleur." I went over to the dresser, near his half-packed bag. Something smelled of ointment.

"I saw you up on that ladder and I know Della's been spying for you."

"What ladder?"

"Come off it. Now, deny you weren't scrounging around the rooftop one night. Deny it. Pretty cheap trick, wasn't it?"

He took out a toothpick and hung it on his lip.

"Wasn't it? That ladder was a waste of time, wasn't it? I could have told you nothing's locked up around here."

In slow patent-leather steps he came towards me; lamplight clung to his toes like fireflies. "Nothing's locked up?" he asked, spraying me with his mint breath.

"What *you* want is locked up. I've seen to that, thank you. Now, what about Della?"

"What about her?"

"Are you meeting her or aren't you? What about Chicago?"

He went back to the window. "What's it to you? Didn't know you were so chummy with her."

"Answer me."

But he wouldn't; he just stood there letting that toothpick roll up and down the loops of his lips.

In his bag: occult magazines, crisp-fresh underwear (Aunt Harry's ironing—not Della's), midnight-blue socks, pills, sandalwood incense, an electric shaver, a wallet. "They know," I said. "I told them—Jerome about the ladder. We've all got your number and we're watching every minute."

"What did you tell them?"

"I told them."

He squeezed his nose and laughed. "You told them. But what's there to tell?" And then, with his cold goose paw, he patted my chin and said, "Besides, you'd have to have some pretty strong evidence to turn those two old bitches against me."

Blood rushed up to my face and I wanted to do harm! The bastard could steal maybe, and do fake spiritual stuff, but I wasn't going to let him get away with being vicious about Aunt Harry and Mrs. Klein. And flaunting it! His bag. On the dresser. Open. Vulnerable. I intended to dump it over and spill his quackeries on the floor to his feet, to humiliate him, but I'd just begun to shove when I remembered the wallet on top of his electric shaver. I grabbed that instead and made a dash towards the door.

"Give that to me!"

One hand was in the doorknob and the other held high his wallet, my prize. "Don't come near. I'll run downstairs with it. You stay right where you are."

Wheezing from his nose. His face alabaster.

"Ransom," I told him, glancing up at the bulging addresses and papers and identifications stuffed in the wallet. "You get this back when you leave this property. Understand, LeFleur? If you so much as do *one* thing against them—to Mrs. Klein or Aunt Harry—if—if you so much as take *one* silver spoon, the police will know how to get in touch with you. Understand? You get this back when you leave. Understand?"

We stood there in duet—he leaning forward, frozen, gripping the edge of the dresser, and I ready to escape down the hall should he make a break towards me. A new wave of blood rushed to my head now that I had complete control over him. The sonofabitch wouldn't dare carry out any foul business now. He looked as though I'd kicked him.

"If you do one bit of harm to those ladies, LeFleur, that'll be your ass." The fat wallet grew greasy, calf-warm, in my sweating hand, and I goaded him, "Warlock, indeed."

He must have thought I was holding his soul from his reach: his rabbit eyes blinked and his adam's apple bobbed and the toothpick shook on his lip like a fang. But soon the moisture on his lips went dry and the toothpick fell, ticking softly when it hit the bulb in the lamp. His hand, that goose paw, flittered around on the dressing table, but his eyes held fast to the confiscated wallet.

Scissors! He lifted them up, inch by inch, but I fled, leaping down the stairs three and four at a time as fear, more than gravity, propelled me downward, away from the warlock with a pair of baby scissors in his hand.

In the backyard, when my heart quieted, I yelled, hopelessly I knew, out through the black grove of trees, *"Della! Della!"* and so shouted along with me the crickets, faster, higher, fiercer, but she would not hear me nor would she hear the crickets; by now she was crossing the highway where the big trucks rolled to Chicago; she probably had just reached the motel, with her valises, smelling of Turkish Kiss Kologne.

I felt rotten as hell and I certainly had little stomach for a tacky séance, but I left the backyard anyway and started for the living room. On the way, as I passed the pantry, I noticed the door was still ajar. Inside a naked bulb swayed, throwing off flashes of yellow into the dark passageway outside. I heard Aunt Harry giggle. She said:

"It burns when it goes down."

"Don't take such big gulps, Harriet dear. Just nip at it."

"How?"

"Watch . . . a little nip . . . a little at a time. Like this. It's not like coffee or tea, dear."

"Here, Etta, let me, let me try again."

"Now careful, Harriet. Just a *bit* at a time."

"Why! Why, Etta, it tastes just like persimmons."

"No such thing."

"It does, it does to me. I know what it tastes like to me."

"I think more like burnt wood, Harriet."

"Burnt wood? How do you know what burnt wood tastes like? You ever tasted burnt wood? Persimmons, I say."

"Well . . . I do think that's enough, don't you? For now? Really, you ought not overdo it, Harriet. I mean—"

"Just one more little nip. One very small little nip, Etta. All right?"

"All right, but I really think— No, no, not so *much*, Harriet."

"Nonsense. It's not as much as you've got. Not even half as much."

"But careful. I drink it all the time. I—I—oh, really Harriet, you're doing more than nipping."

"What do you mean? That was a nip."

"It was more than a nip. Dear, I only wanted you to— to ex*peri*ment. I didn't—Harriet, I told you don't drink it so fast! *Nip.* Merely nip it."

"I was nipping."

"No, you weren't. And look! You dribbled some on top of the cabinet. For goodness' sake, don't waste it."

"I did not dribble, Etta."

"You did so dribble, Harriet Gibbs, I was looking dead at you."

"And I say I didn't dribble. I ought to know if I dribbled or not."

"You did dribble."

"I didn't."

The pantry bulb swayed a bit, with sin, as I sneaked by and went into the living room.

Patricia Jo, turning magazine pages with jerky little flips, jumped as I came in. "Oh! Oh, it's you. Where on earth is Mother Klein and your aunt? Where is everybody? Where is Mr. LeFleur?"

"He's in his room," I told her, and I also said, though she was too jittery to hear: "Mrs. Klein and Aunt Harry are getting pissed in the pantry."

LeFleur's ink hair was plastered across his canopy head, and as he sat he licked his lips. A plain Irish linen covered the dining room table, and on it one candle burned in the middle.

"Sit down, Oliver," Mrs. Klein said nervously. "Sit down. He's going to start."

I had rather expected to see—I don't know what exactly—equipment, I guess. The lights were out and the curtains were drawn and the burning candle gave a certain macabre atmosphere—if that is what he sought; but as I sat, it seemed more like a tranquil dinner party without plates or silverware. LeFleur closed his eyes as soon as I sat down and told us to do the same, and then he placed his goose paws flat upon the table. He sat in this position so long that even I felt perhaps he was in some mysterious trance, but more logically I decided he was saying a very long prayer that he could pull off some credible fakery. Then he spoke, his eyes still closed: "If he comes, if he speaks, it will be to you, Mrs. Klein, only to you. You must tell us what he says. You, you, you must."

So, that's the bastard's ace card! So that's his *modus operandi*! Presumably (O LeFleur! LeFleur!) if the mood was right, if concentration was stretched to the limit, Mrs. Klein would hear—think she would—anything she wanted. There was more than a chance that because the focus was upon her, that because she was ultimately the real star in the matter (not Sargeant, not LeFleur, not her arch rival, Aunt Harry), and because she was inclined to deal in the supernatural, she probably *would* think Sargeant was seeking her. And, too, there was a good heaping measure of charlatanism in Mrs. Klein (it takes one to find one!) that undoubtedly LeFleur had recognized. I questioned whether she would, when hearing nothing from the Other World, admit such a defeat. It was very possible for her to carry the defeat around in her heart, but I wondered if she would pass up the chance to perform, if not to Patricia Jo, then certainly to Aunt Harry. Oh! the clever bastard! His stay at Green Acorns had not been for naught; he knew their pulse beats, their machinations; that had not escaped him. He had, in effect, nothing to do; he could place his goose paws on the table and make Mrs. Klein perform for his fee.

Jerome's hands on the linen looked soft and pink, like Mrs. Klein's, and they trembled; Patricia Jo's were taunt, composed, and they seemed as though they were waiting for cards at a bridge game; Aunt Harry's hands were very black in the candlelight, and I thought I saw, for an instant, an impatient drumming of her fingers.

Accompanied by a lot of deep breathing and Madame Floraism, Mrs. Klein said, "He's coming, Mr. LeFleur, he's coming." She was lying in her teeth. "I think he's coming."

"You think," Aunt Harry muttered, her eyes closed in keeping with the rules of the game.

"Shut up, Harriet," Mrs. Klein replied, eyes closed, with a pleased little smile. "This isn't your affair."

It was a most unfortunate remark. It struck iron-hot. The room sizzled and Aunt Harry jumped up from the table, turning over her chair. "It *is* my affair! It *is* my affair! Sargeant was my baby. He was mine, do you hear!" She ran to the light switch and snapped on the overhead light, revealing a distorted pony face. "He was *mine* and you can't take that away from me!"

"The woman's insane," Mrs. Klein said, hoping we took Aunt Harry's remark literally.

"Oh, yes," Aunt Harry said, advancing, "yours in blood, but mine in spirit and heart and soul." She came over and blew out the candle with a mean little puff and picked up her chair. "'I think he's coming'—indeed! It'd be me he'd be coming to anyway. He was mine, I tell you. That boy was mine all along. I knew what he thought, I knew what he said, I knew why he killed hisself."

Although Aunt Harry's fury and hysteria carried along with it a ring of honesty, Mrs. Klein said, "Nonsense, nonsense. She's losing her mind. She's retarded. She's unbalanced."

Patricia Jo pulled back Aunt Harry's chair. "Sit down, now, sit down, now," she said, her mouse eyes on Aunt Harry, waiting.

"It's the same thing all over again," Mrs. Klein said. "Just as she tries to take credit for you two," she said, bowing her head towards Jerome and Patricia Jo, "she's trying to make Sargeant hers. She should have had children of her own. I know her tricks."

"Mother!" Jerome said, and turned his bloodshot eyes to Aunt Harry. "If you really know, Mrs. Gibbs, you'd better tell us."

"Mrs. Gibbs, Mrs. Gibbs. Ha. Harriet can't even see through that old trick yet."

"Mother!"

"Maybe," Maurice LeFleur said, very cautiously for him, "we could have some refreshments while we hear this." His congeniality took a sharp spurt upwards now that he was no longer master of ceremonies.

"That's enough from you," Aunt Harry told him. "You probably won't want any refreshments when you hear about my poor Sargeant. My baby . . ."

Jerome was getting impatient and Mrs. Klein refused to look at Aunt Harry.

"What precisely?" said Patricia Jo.

Aunt Harry folded her hands and placed them on the table. "He had a sickness, my baby did."

Mrs. Klein snorted. "Sargeant was healthy. He was never sick. See, you can tell she's lying already."

"Mother!" Jerome said.

"He had a sickness of the heart and a sickness of the soul, Sargeant had. And he—"

"Foot, Harriet. You're being dotty and romantic. Oliver, dear, fetch me my rum."

Jerome squeezed his mother's wrist and said, "Good Christ, Mother, can't you be quiet just for a minute? Just for one minute? Good Christ."

"Go on," Patricia Jo begged.

Aunt Harry, who now indisputably had the floor, raised her voice in sermon tones and began her story. "My poor baby had a sickness and a curse and he couldn't marry, he told me, and in New York City he loved a boy."

A glass full of rum flew across the table towards Aunt Harry's face. The glass went over her shoulder, hit the carpet without breaking, but the brown liquid splattered and slid down Aunt Harry's high starched collar.

She did not move. She did not wipe away the rum. She stared straight across the room into space. "Yes, Etta, he loved a boy."

Jerome was standing, holding his mother's shoulders down, and Maurice LeFleur put his elbows on the Irish linen, to listen clinically.

"He took him out of the Morris Mountain Therapy baths in Harlem," Aunt Harry said, staring into the past, her hands now on her lap, her neck stiff. Her story ran on in spurts and digressions with tangential and moral comments, with rationalizations, and her story was peppered with hundreds of mispronunciations. (The St. Regis Hotel, where the Kleins stayed when away from Long Island, was consistently called the St. Regent's; East Sixty-Fourth Street often became North Sixty-Fourth Street; Four Roses whiskey became Red Roses—but then, Mrs. Klein had often been guilty of this misnomer, too; distances shrank and expanded—a taxi trip from the St. Regis to Sutton Place, where there in a bathtub Sargeant slashed his wrists, would cost $4 at one time and 75¢ another; Central Park, referred to as "that nice little park in the middle of town," became a tiny patch of ground one might easily get through with a skip and a jump; Fire Island became the Fire Beach; restaurants and nightclubs that I'd never seen during my two brief visits to Manhattan had such cacophonous names that I'm sure she made them up right on the spot; plays and operas were equally distorted: *The Death of Lady Butterfly*—Sargeant had apparently told her the plot of Puccini's opera—came from her lips with a straight face, and *The Glasses in the Manger* turned out to be, I gathered, after strenuous manipulation, a movie version of *The Glass Menagerie*; and there were other disarrangements ad infinitum.)

These distortions, one suspected, crept into the fact of her narration as well, yet it wasn't vaguely possible she could have made it all up: she spun too many decadent details, too many demimondeisms for a god-fearing lady of her sheltered years. This alone, in spite of her inaccuracies and mutilations, gave a chilling credence to her story, recited in a high, sermon voice.

I began sorting and rearranging her painful rhapsody: it seemed that the hero of the hour had sinister things wrong with his id, or his libido, or both, and visited a Harlem steam bath and brought to his apartment, after lust was spent, an uncouth but particularly handsome colored boy named Roy Flynn. A Pygmalion situation began immediately and Sargeant single-handedly, according to Aunt Harry, transformed Roy Flynn from an ill-mannered, stupid oaf into an urbane creature who—miraculously, it all seemed to me—began feeding upon the likes of Puccini, Braque, Pirandello, and Beerbohm. The creature, this Roy Flynn, it seemed, enjoyed the merits of expensive restaurants and developed a passion for antiques. In fact, Sargeant's life was apparently rotting with contentment until a Mr. T. Geoffrey Collingwood came over from London with a thin blond mustache and with his Mayfair ways. (Mr. Collingwood's name was altered at various points to J. Geoffrey Collingwood, to T. Gregory Collingwood, and to T. J. Collingwood.) And he, the Englishman, if one can believe Aunt Harry's interpretation, "turned all of Sargeant's work to straight-out Sin." The detailed descriptions of the emotional and material transfers from Sargeant to Collingwood, from Collingwood to Sargeant, etc., seesawed the mind. The whole business seemed sordid and dull, but Aunt Harry spoke about it with tears in her eyes.

"Roy Flynn, he took this nice little watch off his wrist—Sargeant gave him the watch. He always gave Roy Flynn things. And he handed this watch to Sargeant like it was the dirtiest thing in the world and he said some smart alecky things that would burn your ears. He had no respect. Even me. I'd come from Long Island to do up Sargeant's Sutton Place place and there this—this awful child would be, ranting at poor Sargeant. And he paid me no mind. Treated me like dirt. Never half covered hisself up. Sometimes wearing them jocket pants *right in front of me.* He liked to show off his body, that vain wicked child from the slums did. That was the trouble—he was slum through and through. In spite of those put-on manners and all that big talk about Strinnervinsky and those picture books of paintings by Frenchmen. No respect, I tell you. He'd walk past me in his jocket pants to fix hisself a drink—even at *eleven o'clock in the morning*—and not as much give me the time of day. Stepping all over my cleaning things. Oh, *some*times that creature would speak, but it was always a sort of uppity 'Good morning, Granny, how's old granny today?' Then again, he wouldn't mumble a word. Disrespect. His disrespect had no end. For instance, when he was having a fight and leaving Sargeant to go off with Mr. T. J. Collingwood, he'd fuss right in front of me like I was a piece of furniture. And he was like honey in the tooth when he came running back to Sargeant's Sutton Place place."

The Harlem Adonis, it seemed, departed and returned rather regularly—a sort of shuttle—but Sargeant was not strong enough to put an end to the ludicrous reconciliations, and things came to an even more shabby circumstance when Roy Flynn began bringing back to Sargeant's place *personae* for mass exhibitions and group participations that were similar, Aunt Harry declared, to Roman orgies (her idea of Roman orgies being based, I dare say, on one or two biblical films), but they were called, she was certain, not Roman orgies but bangbangs. Once she brought by on a non-cleaning day some avocados and some clothes she had taken out to Long Island to mend. It was early evening and she let herself in with her key, but she regretted it, she said; the brief glimpse of the preparations for an orgiastic proceeding caused her to drop the avocados all over the floor, and that one glimpse sent her reeling back to Long Island, where she stayed in bed for a week.

(Aunt Harry, however, likes to exaggerate; she could not live without adding at least one embellishment to a fact.)

Nevertheless, the decline and fall of Sargeant's sordid life quickened during the approaching autumn: he discovered he was flagrantly masochistic and looked forward to Roy Flynn's sadistic antics—or so one must deduce. Aunt Harry was irritatingly vague about much she had seen, and this, coupled with her tendency to preach little sermons, nearly obscured the whole point of her story. Yet if this were true—Sargeant's discovery of his psychosis—it didn't seem very logical that it would cause him to worry and drive him to a psychiatrist ("a doctor of the mind with a foreign name"), for it seemed more plausible that the two personalities would certainly find some measure of harmony in their disparate tastes, whereas, to my mind, if both Roy Flynn and Sargeant had been masochistic, there would then have been a serious impasse in their interaction. Aunt Harry, I had to decide, was either mistaken or she was again distorting the facts.

Also, she seemed fascinated with irrelevant details. "I fixed his apartment up as pretty as a picture on New Year's Eve. He was having a party and before I left at nine o'clock or so, just before the first of his guests came, the rubber plant was shining so green and pretty and the black and yellow stones of the coffee table . . ." (She went on, I'm sure, for twenty minutes praising her handiwork—the hors d'oeuvres, the buffet spread.) "But my poor boy was very sad and he hadn't even yet dressed for his own party. He just sat there drinking a glass of something." (Had this been anyone else in the world besides Sargeant, it wouldn't have been a "glass of something"; it would have surely been a "glass of liquor.") "He sat there looking out the window at that big red Biscuit sign on the other side of the river. He confessed on my shoulders, that boy did, on that New Year's Eve before the party. He told me *everything*. He said *I* was his only friend. He said *I* was the only one who could understand him. He said *I* was the only one he could trust. He said *I* was the only one he could pour out his heart to. And he asked me—oh, Lord Jesus, forgive me—not to never tell, never. He asked me that and here I am betraying my baby! And he asked me to forgive him, and I said, 'Sargeant, baby, you don't have to ask Harriet that. You'll never sin in my heart.'

"And he said, 'Just promise to forgive me, please promise.'

"And I said, 'Naturally, I promise. And you promise me to get rid of that no-account Harlem scum.'

"And he said, and he laughed wild as an animal when he said, 'I will Harriet! I will Harriet! Tonight I'll get rid of him for good. Forever I'll get rid of him for good.'

"And I said, 'Glory be' and kissed him and left— around nine-fifteen, before the first guest came, not even knowing he would cut his wrists in the bathtub in the middle of the party in the middle of the night. Oh, Merciful Father, how was I to know my baby was going to cut his wrists in the bathtub in the middle of the night? Jesus, My Lord, O have mercy."

At that moment, there was a Judgment Day, of sorts. Mrs. Klein, still held in her seat by Jerome's big pink hands (he'd stood all the time, frozen), beat her face with her chubby fists and said, with her teeth practically clamped shut, "No! no! It's not true, none of it's true!" Her protestations did not fool anyone; we all knew it was true, more or less, in spite of Aunt Harry's predilection for gilding a lily. "It's not, it's not," she said, weaving and bowing back and forth over the table; and with both fists in the air, as though she were doing a Sophocles drama, she said: "You're an evil, evil, evil woman! A vicious old woman! You're a—a demented old, old—old evil nigger woman!"

Aunt Harry cried.

"I hate you," Mrs. Klein hollered, her head now resting on the table top, her fists hitting the Irish linen around her head.

"Etta, Etta," Aunt Harry sniffed, fiberglass hair falling in her face, "in all these years . . . in all these long years through everything . . . you've never . . . Etta . . ."

"My brother," Jerome whispered, a bit dazed. "He was a fucking queer." Nobody seemed to notice the vulgar word. "My *own* brother! My flesh and blood."

Aunt Harry was crying and Mrs. Klein was banging the table and Jerome was cursing and nobody saw that Patricia Jo was having a strange problem: she didn't seem to be breathing well. The tiny space between her head and shoulders tightened and her head was back on the edge of the straight chair. When she leaned forward, holding her stomach with her hands, I saw that she was laughing—sort of. It was a painful laughing, to be sure, and it obviously gave her no pleasure. Finally she said, "And that's it, and that's it . . . all this time and that's it."

"How *could* he?" Jerome was asking, asking anybody who would answer. "How could he be a faggot?"

Maurice LeFleur seemed embarrassed and uncertain of the victory, uncertain perhaps whether he felt the victory was his or not. He wanted to light his tiny cigar, but he did not, fearing probably it would indicate sacrilege. But he did mumble a sly thing, which I heard and I *believe* Patricia Jo heard: "So, why didn't Sargeant pick a nice Jewish boy?"

Maybe she didn't hear his *sotto voce* remark but her hysteria came, right after that, into full bloom. She laughed, with her teeth attracting everybody's eyes, and she pushed in her stomach as though it pained her.

"Stop that woman!" Mrs. Klein shouted. "Shut that woman up!"

"You made me betray him . . . my baby," Aunt Harry said.

"Patricia Jo?" Jerome said.

"In my bag, I have some—" Maurice LeFleur began and stopped, casting a quick eye over the lot. "Maybe some water?"

"Patricia Jo!" Jerome tapped her laughing cheeks.

"Shut that woman up," Mrs. Klein said, beating on the table with each syllable. Because Jerome had no success with his wife, she yelled at him: "Get that bitch out of here! Get her out!"

"Mother!"

"Etta . . . you called me . . . you said . . ."

And Patricia Jo laughed. Her health seemed as though it would be in danger if she did not stop, but when Jerome slapped her face (as Mrs. Klein screamed "bitch" again), the laughter turned to tears and crying, which had a healthier sound. He led her towards the study and said, "Bring me some brandy, Oliver."

As it turned out I was solicited for a number of chores. Wet towel. Cognac. Handkerchief. Rum. Ash tray for

LeFleur! (He seemed afraid to move from his seat.) Water. Curtains back in place.

On the way with the towel to Patricia Jo in the study, there was:

"Etta, you never called me that in all these years. All these years."

"Hush, Harriet. Hush up, now, dear."

On the way back with the towel to get a glass of water for Patricia Jo, there was:

"You made me betray him, Etta. I didn't want to. I betrayed my baby."

In the study Patricia Jo was quite sober. In fact, dour. "How are you going to fight that, Jerome? Just tell me, how are you? *You can't.* Your mother'll get over it . . . oh, yes, she'll get over it. Mothers always get over it. And then Sargeant will become some kind of martyr, some kind of saint. It's like a dirty trick."

On my way back to the kitchen I saw Mrs. Klein brushing Aunt Harry's hair back from her face.

When I came out of the kitchen, Mrs. Klein was saying, ". . . so don't fret, Harriet, it couldn't be helped. Now, now, dear, take a bitsy nip of the rum."

This did not surprise me; I was by now used to their chameleonic behavior: they could clash swords one minute and the next they would be kissing; they could compose poison letters to each other one minute and request papal dispensations for each other the next. I'd learned not to try to keep track. But I had a fear: their eyes, those Rachmaninoff eyes, turned on Maurice LeFleur, and though they held their tongues for the moment, I knew it would not be long before he would become their scapegoat. He was there, he was the logical one. But it could well have been almost anybody, anything. They could not be separated for very long, not seriously separated at any rate, and they would use any means, no matter how outlandish, to get back together—as long as they could save face. Yet, one day, one would have to die, die before the other. What would the surviving one do? They had woven a bickering, bantering tapestry together that was stronger than husband and wife, or sisters or cousins. And this bickering and bantering, this arguing, I was beginning to learn, was not to be made light of; it was a high seriousness, their arguing; it was the way they made love.

But there was still an estrangement, in spite of the soothing words, and it was for this reason I began to feel uneasy about Maurice LeFleur. When I went back into the study, I asked Jerome, "What are you going to do about him? LeFleur?"

"Pay him. Get rid of him. What else? Come on Patricia Jo, it's late. I don't know why you won't stay the night here at Mother's."

"In this house?"

"Now, Mother doesn't mean half of what she—"

"Oh, for goodness' sake, Jerome, can't you see she's going to be worse now? About everything? As long as you don't count, then I count even less. Can't you get that through your thick head? Funny . . . there's no more of the Sargeant ghost now, but it's even worse. Mark my words, he'll turn into a saint. Mark my words."

"Come on," Jerome said, and they both walked back into the dining room, in a dirge walk, to face Maurice LeFleur, to face Mrs. Klein.

"You're leaving?" Mrs. Klein's inquiry was coated with Sweetness and Goodness; she even thought to finger feebly her black buttons. "You really should stay here overnight. It's far too late to be driving back to Kalamazoo."

Jerome shook his head. "No, we should go." He glanced at Maurice LeFleur, who *still* sat at the head of the table. Jerome pulled out a checkbook. "Here's five hundred, LeFleur—for your services. Leave immediately in the morning." And I, in an attempt to underscore Jerome's disdain, dropped LeFleur's wallet, as though it were a leech, into his lap.

Mrs. Klein stood over Aunt Harry with one fat hand resting on top of Aunt Harry's fiberglass hair. They stayed in that position, as though they were waiting for Gainsborough to walk in and paint a portrait of them, and they looked at Maurice LeFleur, watched him put the check in his vest pocket.

He had found a toothpick somewhere, and it was stuck in the corner of his mouth.

5

The Reconciliation Hour took place in the kitchen over a bottle of rum. Aunt Harry drank it (straight!) without wincing, which led me to the inevitable conclusion that she had been drinking all along, drinking on the sly. They sat across from each other, befogged, hardly concerned at all that Della had run off and left a sink full of dishes. ("She would have to go and do a thing like this in our *greatest* hour," Mrs. Klein said.) They refused to look at the ugly pile of dishes in the sink. ("I never did trust that girl," Aunt Harry said. "Bred wrong.")

Because they ignored me quite a bit, and because it was late, I left them sitting there at the kitchen table. I could have forgotten them right away had the tone of their bickering zigzagged along with its usual inflections and with its customary cadences. But something was wrong: they were having a hard time letting so much water go under the bridge. For one thing, Aunt Harry seemed to be on the defensive throughout their needlepoint combat; she seemed, in spite of her triumphant claim on Sargeant, to be the loser, for it was not the tragedy of Sargeant's sordid life that preoccupied their thought, but rather Aunt Harry's betrayal of Sargeant. No matter how many times Mrs. Klein reminded her that it was understandable, that it was necessary under the circumstances—spilling the beans as she did—there was an undisguised glee in Mrs. Klein's voice, and Aunt Harry must have detected it and she must have known that she would never hear the end of it; she probably already heard the words Mrs. Klein would use ("treacherous," "blabbermouth") at some future date, some future time. However, their new crisis seemed incredibly self-centered. Here was their Loved One in his grave because he'd led such a downward life, but those two cared only about their game of squelches—a game neither would win, and a game that would last for eternity. Their indifference was villainous; it was as though they sat over Sargeant's remains picking at each other.

Aunt Harry was as busy as Faust in her attempt to regain her position. She could not stand for her opponent to have one up on her—more than one up on her by the way she was carrying on (influence of rum aside), talking quicker than crickets chatter. Her tactic, it seemed—and I cannot be at all sure, for I was cold-shouldered and hinted to darkly that it was past my bedtime (theirs too, for that matter!), so I left the kitchen, not too graciously, to scout around for a bedtime cigarette—but her tactic, it seemed, was to gain ascendency by assuring Mrs. Klein that Maurice LeFleur was a fake all the time, that she knew that Maurice LeFleur was a quack, a low sort of person out to get anything he could get, and that she just went along with the gag to pacify a doting old matriarch. Well, I wondered how far even Aunt Harry could stretch that one, but I wasn't around to find out.

I did hear occasionally, floating upstairs through the open window in the summer night (morning—it was going on four o'clock)—I did hear things like *Harriet Gibbs*!

And twenty minutes later I heard: *low-down, just plain low-down.*

Then dozing. Later. Ten minutes later? Seconds? Later on I heard: *How a grown woman, lo, these—a woman in her seventies—*

Late sixties.

—in her seventies could be so gullible . . .

Between these exuberant flayings I dozed and sometimes heard the footsteps of Maurice LeFleur, who probably was getting himself ready to go, or he was pacing the floor as he made up his mind whether or not he was going off to teach Della how to be a whore.

Time edged along towards dawn as I dozed and woke, heard footsteps, heard rum-thick voices, and dozed again. At one point, when the outside looked metallic and cold, as though lit by a gray neon light, I got up. I felt affirmative. Authoritative. I thought I would try to make Aunt Harry and Mrs. Klein go to bed. It was insane to drink right through to early morning. But as I was opening my door I heard someone on the stairs—probably they'd decided at last to come to bed. Yet as soon as I prepared to settle down again for serious sleep, I heard the footsteps descend. They were the brittle, impatient steps of Aunt Harry, but I couldn't be sure; the humidity and quiet of coming dawn fogged the senses and clogged the mind.

Doors opened. Doors shut. Upstairs, down. Drawers opened. Shut. Only deaf Bertram had peace. He always slept.

I did, finally—how long? two minutes later? ten?—get up to double check the "Moose at Bay" in the hallway, and I lifted it out enough to see that Mrs. Klein's jewel case was not sitting on the tiny nook in the wall behind the ugly picture. LeFleur could not have known about it. No one knew, not even Della, except me, except Aunt Harry and Mrs. Klein.

When I heard the racket down below, in the back of the kitchen, in the yard, my drowsiness cleared and I ran to my window to see. Outside, where the dawn was turning into oyster colors, there were harsh shouts and I saw below Maurice LeFleur in flight with his black leather bag. Aunt Harry and Mrs. Klein were behind him with sticks, toddling in housecoats—it looked like a speeded-up minuet, that pathetic little chase in the yard, in the dawn. Maurice LeFleur, a butterfly in a suit and vest of midnight blue, made an easy escape, a grin on his face as he turned to raise his free arm in courtly farewell, but—in absurd swiftness—as though the gods resented the Picasso loops of his lips, he stumbled on the salt lick, fell on his face in the joe-pye weeds. Aunt Harry was first on him with a knotty stick, then Mrs. Klein. He hunched up his shoulders, writhed, got on his hands and knees, but fell again under the blows of the heavy sticks over his head, blow after blow, from the ladies above him. It was good to see—at first; he deserved the disgrace. But when he was no longer struggling and lay there, his canopy head in the joe-pye weeds, wet with dew, I began to feel sick in the stomach: the ladies beat on, one after another, like railroad workers pounding spikes. And they continued, as though he were a snake that might spring upon them, as though they were beating something else—not a man, not a snake—as though it were a beating spot. It was inhuman, nonhuman, that beating. *They were not beating a man. They must stop. Please stop. They must stop.*

One of the sticks was tinted red.

"Stop it!" I shouted, but they would not hear me. I ran downstairs to the yard, but he had struggled free, and he was running, leaving behind his black leather bag, towards the grove of trees. They followed, as best the rum allowed them, and with sticks raised high they entered the black grove slashing pell-mell the innocent trees. I could not see into the grove but I heard the crunches beneath their feet, and faintly, in the distance, between the noise of a heavy caravan on the highway, I heard a crackle, almost tender—Maurice LeFleur had made his escape. Yet they stayed on in the grove a bit, hitting tree trunks with their sticks, and then, abruptly, the curve of the sun pushed up into the gray air, at the far end of the earth.

Mrs. Klein's face was blue when she came out of the grove. Aunt Harry's looked ashen, and it seemed to be swelling, and she pushed a hand in tight towards her withered breast. She got ahead of Mrs. Klein and dipped into Maurice LeFleur's bag, which was wet with dew and glistened with the first rays from the sun. "See," she said, holding up the jewel box that encased the Teardrop. "Didn't I tell you he was a robber, too? Didn't I tell you? Lookit," she said, taking out the gaudy necklace, "see what that robber was robbing!"

It was so stilted, her voice. So frightened. It was not a voice I'd heard from her any of my days, and I had not the heart to ask her how did the necklace get there, who took it from behind the picture. I could not prove anything, I could not say anything, I could not indicate my burning suspicion—because—because her hands shook so. Aunt Harry's hands shook so, holding that necklace up in the morning sun to our faces. Her poor hands shook so. Her hands were so eager to demonstrate. So eager. Her hands shook so that I did not see her face. I did not see that she was dying.

"Run, Oliver, her medicine! Run!"

When I returned, I found Mrs. Klein crying, and she said, her pink fists tight, "Oh, Oliver, look what Harriet's done. *Look* what she's done."

She lay still on the ground, near the salt lick.

"Harriet? Harriet? Oh, Oliver, is she dead? Is she dead?"

Sun pushed up and filled my eyes and cocks were crowing and Mrs. Klein pressed her face into my neck and we clung to each other for a long time.

THREE

1

Aunt Harry's funeral was not a success: bushels of yellow-red-purple flowers were there, piled high at her grave, but there were not a dozen people. I don't know exactly what I expected from a funeral—gloom perhaps. Although it was not a festive occasion, there was, none the less, an irreverent amount of gaiety on the part of Nature: red-winged birds cut free-verse poems through the air; the graveyard grass grew vigorously green even as we stood upon it; marble tombstones with round and pointed heads peeked up into the afternoon sun for acres around us to watch our ceremony; a caretaker at the far south of us snipped a row of shrubs with silver shears, whistling a peppy tune; Mrs. Klein was deep in a veil, and the sky was Sibelius blue.

Jerome was a businessman as well as a sentimentalist; not only did he take care of the funeral matters with admirable efficiency, he decided also that Aunt Harry and his mother would be buried side by side. He knew full well they had husbands and graveyard plots of their own, but he did not hesitate to dismiss these facts, and he prepared to commit this one great sentimental act, and because of it, I forgave him for every coarse, irritating thing he had ever done. (I did wonder, however, what Ezra Klein and Gideon Gibbs, wherever they were, would think of such an unorthodox arrangement.) It surprised me to discover that one's enemy, or near-enemy, also could have a streak of nobility, have a worthy heart. His one decision, like a very sharp knife, cut away a coarse husk to reveal a bright kernel.

Although no one told her, Mrs. Klein must have guessed that the spot next to Aunt Harry's would one day hold her: her veiled face hung over the unused space next to Aunt Harry's grave during the entire service at the cemetery. She stood quietly. She did not once cry.

Among the condolences on the foyer table at Green Acorns (a sympathy note from the twins, Mark and Marcus) there was a letter for me. It was postmarked Chicago, Ill.

DEAR OLIVER,

Where in the goddam hell is Maurie? He still there? Has that bastard up and ditched me? Can you beat that? I waited at that ratty motel until god knows how long and I figgered it made no sense to hang around and just spend more money. So, this here man had a new station wagon with a radio in it who dint move me none at all, but he was going to Chicago and I started to getting nervous like anything after Maurie dint show up so I jumped a ride with him and told him I dint want no smart stuff and he said he was a gentleman and wouldn't start no smart stuff and he dint lay a finger on me until we got to Chicago. He cussed me out good and proper because he expected something for that ride he gave me. That dirtie dog. I'm staying at the St. James Hotel for Ladies and Gentlemen so have your auntie to send my pay here. I need it bad. And if I ever see that Maurie I'm going to fix his wagon for good I can tell you that. LOVE. DELLA.

PS. My address is The St. James Hotel For Ladies and Gentlemen, Room Number 201. LOVE. DELLA.

I cried and I meant to be laughing. I thought I was laughing, but I wasn't, and when Mrs. Klein's nurse caught me at it, she patted my back and kept telling me it was good for me to cry and she made me some soup. (She was a real Soup Woman; in her mind, it cured everything. It wasn't soup I needed. I didn't know what I needed, for I tried to stop thinking, about everything, especially about Sargeant.) And it was no good showing her the letter. It was no good showing anybody the letter. I tore it up, and tore up my summer poem about the Shetland ponies on a beach, and walked around the house wishing it was already time to go to Ithaca.

Mrs. Klein began staying in bed the whole day, and when she did get up she wouldn't talk. Even Jerome was stingy with words. I never knew it was so hard to kill time. What fun was it watching the goddamned bluejays? I was tired of Baudelaire. Sargeant! Damn you, Sargeant!

•

How did time go? How was it used up? There was in the afternoons always the drone of bees.

One evening I read nine pages of Wordsworth poems to Mrs. Klein. She did not stroke PG, who sat in her lap, nor did she ask me to repeat any word. I read every other line, skipped over lines, and she did not stir. I read the poems backwards, in a serious voice, and found it amused me. For a while. I said good night, but she did not reply, nor did she nod.

Nighttimes, crickets would chatter. Out by the black grove of trees.

Wednesday, I got another letter from Della. There was no return address.

DEAR OLIVER,

For about a week or more I been with the Salvation Army people and they love my voice. Just love it. They sure are a corny bunch of bastards but I can't knock it I guess because at least I'm eating and I get to see some parts of this city I would of never seen before I guess, only I'm getting bored and hot to get on with my plans. I think I'll be able to get a good job with a lady who has got a good house and a good business and this lady says I'll be a good addition because they don't have my type in her house. (They got a high yellow colored girl there, but she acts funny and foreign.) You know something? I thought I saw Maurie last week in the place they call the Loop and I ran two long blocks bumping into people trying to get to him and I was embarrassed out of my mind when I found out it wasn't him. I'm still BITTER AS HELL about how he ditched me! Believe me, I'm going to catch up with that s.o.b. if it is the last thing I do, and when I do brother he better watch out. I'm not kidding because I don't forget. That goddam dirtie dog. And I'm getting pretty hot over your auntie too. I'm suppose to get pay for those days irregardless if I did leave like that and you tell her if I don't get it soon I'm going to write the Better Business Buro people and that'll put some steam under her I bet. I sure need some clothes and things to fix up. It's awful. Other people have pretty things and I'm a mess. Sometimes I get sick in the stomach just thinking about it. LOVE. DELLA.

PS. I haven't had The Nasties even once since I been here. Isn't that the kicks?

2

"Harriet?" She turned sharply as I came in the living room. "Harriet, is that you?" Her hand poked up through the sleeve of her Academy of Dramatic Arts dressing gown and she whispered. Over and over, she whispered to herself.

"She's away, Mrs. Klein," I told her in a low voice, wondering if she meant me to answer. "You remember, Aunt Harry's gone away."

A drone from bees rose up to the open window, and there at the window the sun passed by, going down. She looked at the edge of the sun brushing the oak trees for a while, then she beckoned to me with her pink chubby hand. "Listen," she whispered, pulling me down to reach my ear, "she's hiding," and then, having shared with me her secret knowledge, she folded her arms in a minute's contentment. "But I know all the places in this house. All the places. Better than she knows the places."

I hated to treat her as though she were a child; whatever she'd been to me, she'd never been a child. Yet . . . to play with her a game of hide-and-seek. Some of the old blue fire came into her eyes as she began to get up, get out of her cushioned chair. "Harriet," she snapped, looking right, looking left, waiting for a reply. Only the drone from bees answered; only a crush of oak in the wind answered. "I'm too old for this nonsense," she said, standing up. "Stop hiding—it's disgraceful for a woman of your age."

"Mrs. Klein, Mrs. Klein, please."

"Stop hiding, I say. Stop it, stop it." She walked around the chair with new energy, stealing glances at the Chinese Chippendale cabinet near the bay window; she didn't like the looks of it; she looked at it from the side of her face, advancing towards it, slowly, but looking at it with her face averted, from a far corner of her eye. Then, up to the Chinese Chippendale, but not too close, she said, in careful phrases, "Come out of there, Harriet."

I tried to stop her but she spatted my hand, just as Aunt Harry use to spat hands.

"Nurse! Nurse!" I shouted, which brought, marching in her starch, the nurse into the room. Nothing perturbed the middle-aged nurse: she had strong arms and quick fingers and she had pills to make people sleep. She could rule the world if she wanted to.

"Come," she said, putting Mrs. Klein's arm into a grip that made Mrs. Klein's eyes look up in strange wonder. "Now be calm. Sit down." Her voice sounded unfriendly. "You will have to go to bed again if you tire yourself out running around." The nurse stood there a minute, probably thinking she should put Mrs. Klein in bed anyway, but then she knew her patient had spent too much time there already. Instead of guiding her upstairs, she said, "You'll get some soup," thinking, I'm sure, that soup cured everything.

"Stay here with her," she told me and marched out in starch to fetch the soup.

But Mrs. Klein wouldn't take her eyes off the Chinese Chippendale and soon she began pounding the arm of the chair with her fist—knocking Aunt Harry's crocheted doily to the floor. "I know you. You're in there with Sargeant. I know you two." She stopped beating her fist on the chair, but she wouldn't take her eyes away from the cabinet. "Sargeant," she said, her voice half lost in the whip of leaves of the trees, "you and Harriet come right out of there."

"Here's your soup," the nurse said, putting it down nearby, "but first—" She wrapped a band around Mrs. Klein's arm and then squeezed a rubber ball attached to the apparatus. There was no telling from the nurse's face the condition of Mrs. Klein's blood pressure, but it could not have been far wrong, for she merely said, "Eat your soup," and right away she left, dragging behind her the mysterious instrument.

"Soup," Mrs. Klein said meanly, exhibiting in her expression of distaste a strength I thought had forever left her. "Goddamned soup," she said, glaring at it. And this unnerved me, hearing her swear so naturally, and hearing her express so vividly my exact sentiments. But I would have never turned up the bowl like that—as she did, with such graceful premeditation—so that its contents would spill to the floor. Chopped carrots and soft potatoes fell, like lethargic marbles, over the carpet at our feet.

"Now, now," I said, perversely pleased at this display of temper; at least she was alive again; it was better than lying still in cotton sheets watching bluejays fly away.

"I know they're in that cabinet and I'm going to get in that cabinet." She advanced, taking the soup spoon with her as if it were her weapon.

"Mrs. Klein, wait. Wait, I'll open it. Wait."

"Well, open it, then," she said, beating the Chinese Chippendale with her spoon. "I'm tired of their games, I'm tired of their games. You hear me in there?"

Yet when I opened the cabinet, filled with linen and long candlesticks, it did not seem to placate her; she merely turned towards the bay window, with her spoon, and said, "They're always against me, those two. They're always playing games against me."

The cabinet doors were open. I left them open. I did not know what to do. I did not know what to do. I could not think. I could only feel the breeze from the great oak trees. A gust, now and then, lifted the sleeves of Mrs. Klein's dressing gown, beating her softly about her face, and caught up in a dance were the faded blue folds at her feet. On each of these gusts of oak tree wind came the smell of honeysuckle and the smell of far-off rain, and she stood in the middle of it, stood giddy and light, rowing her fingers through the fragrance as though she were tickling water. Back and forth she touched the texture of the wind as she hummed to herself a song without words. Soon her feet began to move beneath the gown. Soon her voice sounded of music, high, fluted, as she talked in quick patches so that she might not disturb the oak wind. At first it was difficult to hear what she said; only the words "summer" and "brocatelle" filtered through. Once it seemed she said "Molière," but for this I could not fashion a logic, but then I could not clearly think, standing as I was in enchanted fright, watching the figures she made, the half circles of a somnolent pavane, with an oak-blown smile on her lips. The carpet caught her slipper—a beach fluff with sheepskin—but she would not take heed of it, continuing her half-step dance without one shoe, waving her fingers in rivers of wind. "I was beautiful, very beautiful once," she said, dancing alone in the breeze. "In the summer of thirty-three. Remember, Harriet, in thirty-three, the orchard and the beach? And you, you with that silly Chantilly lace. Summer, summer. A summer of tulle, and all those trees by the lake and lace." She laughed high, not her mahogany rifle shots, but high, and over the wind. "I had no patience with your needles and yarn. Oh, the way you made things with needles and yarn when the summer was full of grace! Pomegranates and ice. And breeze from the sea. And you, you with your needles and yarn."

She turned to Aunt Harry's chair and bowed, in a queenly fashion. "You remember, Harriet, the summer of thirty-three? I used to dance, but did I dance in the summer of thirty-three? Ah," she whispered as Bertram entered, acknowledging him, or acknowledging Maximilien François Marie Isidore de Robespierre, or the King of Iceland, or a midsummer night's court. Bertram saw the blue and the glaze of her eyes and swallowed the question on his lips. And bit by bit his stone face cracked into wrinkles and he held those wrinkles there, as if a shield to the sight of Mrs. Klein's tilting dance in the wind. Still, he came forward, slowly, as if to grab her, to press to her sides the gentle flays of her gown about her, but he stopped and they did not touch. They stood face to face. Only the sleeve of her gown touched, and it touched him for a second, as if to caress him, as if to greet him, but they did not speak. Outside, the crescendo from the rattle of oak drowned out the drone from the bees.

"Bombay gin and Pericles," she said, but it could not have meant anything—unless it meant everything. They were now back to back, a yard apart, standing as statues midst the currents from the great oaks. "Have they all gone to Saratoga again, Harriet?" Her voice rose in operatic delight. "Have they all gone away?"

With that query still hanging high in the air, the spell was broken and they, still back to back, parted to the other sides of the room—she blissful and content, lifting her face to get a honeysuckle kiss, and he, silent, holding fast to the mantle, with tight-hunched shoulders, holding fast to the mantle.

When Mrs. Klein raised her arms, shooting them like rockets through her sleeves, and when she said, "Wind sailing, wind wailing, O summer wind," Bertram made a move towards the door: one step, two steps. His hand clutched objects, furniture, as a blind man feeling his way through a foreign room. His face was close to the wall. When Mrs. Klein laughed, a high summer laugh, and said, "Tell them, Harriet, that every bit of it was true," Bertram continued his groping movements, near the Wedgwood vase, near the broken lowboy, to make his way out of the room.

I couldn't stand the sight any longer. Bertram would be choking up and crying, and of course to see *him* cry would be enough to start me up, and Jesus Christ, it had become a house of crying—Aunt Harry crying and shrill Patricia Jo crying and Della with gold piercing her ear crying, and

Jesus, all I needed was for Bertram to start crying . . . I took quickly to the window, to close the window, to set myself in action.

"No, no, Sargeant." Mrs. Klein came to touch the windowpane. "I like the summer wind." Her blue eyes looked straight through me. "Harriet, come over here and make Sargeant open the window. Harriet? Harriet, where'd you go again?"

A vaseline glass crashed down from a bric-a-brac stand as Bertram left the room. His hands still groped along before him in the hallway, those hard-iron hands, as though he were blind, as though he were in a rage, as though he dared not trust his feet to navigate alone.

But quickly the hysteria came to a halt: with plenty of energy to spare, Mrs. Klein stepped around the spilled soup, arranged her gown, plucked at the folds gone askew, and sat down in her chair. She sat there in stern decorum, simply, and her eyes were now a tranquil blue, just as though there had been no disarray. "Would you mind reading a bit of Wordsworth to me?"

My delight was complete, for I took this request as a healthy sign, and I ran up to her room to get the poems I hated, but now, oh, now! wished ever to read.

The pain, though, returned when I came back to the living room and found her, there on the floor, on her hands and knees, trailing a broken strand of beads around the soup on the floor. *"How long, how long, have that evenin' train been gone."* She was singing Della's song, her hands and knees lost in the folds of her dressing gown.

"Oh, Mrs. Klein, oh, Mrs. Klein," I said like some silly ass, too shaken to pry her away from her game. The beads continued their journey around the soup and she continued to sing Della's song.

"Jerome! Jerome!" I shouted at the top of my lungs, which brought him thumping and thundering, three steps at a time, down the stairs.

"What? *Mother.*" He blushed a quick red and ran to kneel at her side. "Where's the nurse? Nurse!" he called but there did not come the sound of her march of starch. "The bitch is probably out there eating soup."

Even Jerome had become anti-soup. "Come on, Mother," he said, taking away her bead-train, "let's get up. Let's go upstairs to bed."

"How long," she asked gently, "have that evenin' train been gone?"

"What?"

"It's Della's song," I told him.

"Where's that goddamn nurse?" Jerome asked again, lifting Mrs. Klein from the floor.

But she wiggled and pulled away. Although she had to lean on his arm for support, she protested, and said, "No." She shook her head and said "No" again.

"But you need to get to bed, Mother. Now come on, be good." He reached to lift her once again and she pulled away. "Mother, please."

She caught her breath and looked at me. "I want Sargeant to take me to my room. Sargeant can take—"

"Mother, you know Sargeant isn't here. You know better, Mother."

But Mrs. Klein took a step towards me and held out her hand. "Sargeant, you will take me up to my room. Can you carry me up, Sargeant?"

The sorrow on Jerome's face was awful to see. I looked away and wished I were not there. "Sargeant . . ."

"Well, what in the hell you waiting for, Oliver?" He waved his freckled hand in my face, snorting. "We've got to get her up to bed. Nurse! Nurse! I'm going to fire that bitch."

She was light, although the gown was cumbersome and it clung over everything as I carried her towards the stairs.

"Sargeant . . ." she said in a low music.

Jerome's face twitched every time his mother spoke. He followed us up, one step at a time, slowly. "I love you, too, Mama." He was puffing and reaching out to touch the folds of his mother's gown. "I love you, too."

"How long, how long . . ."

"Mama! Don't you hear, Mama?"

"Sargeant, I knew all along you were hiding. Weren't you?"

"Mama!"

"I'm sorry, Jerome," I said. "I'm, I'm—"

"Nurse! Where is she? Mama? Oh damn oh damn oh damn. Nurse! Mama? Don't you know I love you, too, Mama? Don't you?"

I looked over my shoulder, with some of Mrs. Klein's hair in my eyes. "I'm really sorry about this, Jerome. I mean, I—"

"For crissake keep going. Just get her to bed. Just get her to bed. Mama?" he called behind us, in a voice hardly audible, by the banister, at the landing of the top of the stairs. He did not follow us to her room.

He stood there.

3

In the attic I searched for Sargeant's trunk.

I was not sure I would find it, or anything of his, for I had never explored this cobwebbed region of Green Acorns, nor had I ever had the desire to do so. What I expected to find was not clear to me, but it was an activity that came close to relieving the panic I'd been pushing away. My search was encumbered by the numerous debris—every conceivable object the household had stuck away for safekeeping or openly admitted was ready for disposal. Occasionally, sharp pains of grief would come as I picked up a hideous old hat of Aunt Harry's, or stumbled into a picnic basket she had once filled with food to take to Lake Michigan. But one could cope with pain; far worse was fear: *I did not know where to find that which I did not know I was seeking.* It was like playing blindman's buff alone. There was, of course, enough reason left in my heated movements to sort out one fact: I had become a victim of Sargeant's death. Perhaps the grief belonged to Mrs. Klein and to Aunt Harry, but ultimately I was the victim; he had robbed me of whatever

I had had, whatever I had been. In spite of all my protestations that I was Oliver, Oliver, Oliver, and not this
Sargeant person, there was now with the discovery of his
mystery a void in what I'd come to call my life. Whatever
shaky foundations I had had beneath me, no matter how
false it may have been, was, after all, a foundation, it
was something on which to start. I cannot deny that
I was inordinately proud of my learning—my French,
my Tolstoy, my Kierkegaard—and that my tutors had
filled me with knowledge beyond my years, had made
me a peer in my graduating class. But it did not seem to
work too well with living. I was not, of course, trying to
be Sargeant, nor had I ever entertained the notion, but
now—and it seemed suddenly—that he was no longer a
mere name, I had, so that I might know who I was, to find
out what *their* image of him was—Mrs. Klein's, Patricia
Jo's, Jerome's. I felt that could I see their image of him,
I could see how that image was being welded onto me,
and perhaps I could see what I—am? was? It was crazy:
at nearly seventeen, armed with irregular verbs and philosophy, I was thrashing around a dirty attic looking for
myself. Looking for myself! And it was a terror to feel a
body, the body of me, searching in half panic for—for—
suppose I did not exist! Suppose I did not exist! Suppose
there was nothing to be found, after nearly seventeen
years, it—the body searching in the attic—was a mere
flesh-and-blood thing. And that flesh-and-blood thing
searching in the attic could appear in a room, in a world,
the same as a table, the same as a chair. Suppose I did
not exist! What proof did I have that I did? Chair-chair.
Oliver-Oliver. By giving it a name—did that make it

be? Where had I been all of my life and where was I now—the *me* part, housed in this flesh and blood? Where was it now? Could I have secretly thought, as I stood on soapboxes denouncing the séance, that I would see this horror: this horror of not knowing, of nothingness? Looking back, I now seemed a hysterical boor, ranting on about a tacky necklace, even if that ranting had been disguised in the respectable cloak of logic. What had I been resisting? *Becoming* me or *discovering* me? My hand. My hand loomed larger and larger upon the dusty chair. It was there. A hand. Without belonging. On the dirty chair. It was not my hand; it was *a* hand, a hand in the world, a hand on the chair. It—like the rest of the body— could not belong, could not be, until there was something to belong to, until it would know how to be.

I stood there feeling naked and ashamed, for my murky philosophy had turned to self-pity and I found that I had, for some time, been crying, and in disgust I knocked over lamps and dress models to continue my search. And at last, a quarter of an hour later, I found a rather small box, tied in a wrapping cord, marked: Sargeant S. Klein. The handwriting on the box was Aunt Harry's and so was the tough sailor's knot that surrounded it.

I was fearful of my booty: I shook as though I had palsy and was afraid to open the box; it seemed alive; it seemed a Pandora's box; it also seemed to be waiting for me.

Its harmless contents turned me into a silly laughing goat, and I spread dust and sneezed.

Metropolitan Opera programs. New York City Ballet programs. Slender volumes of poems translated from the Japanese. Three Ronald Firbank novels. A box with a

number of odd cuff links, tie pins. Two little finger rings.
A Phi Beta Kappa key. A manila envelope stuffed with
pornographic pictures. And a picture—God! circa 1930!—
of Aunt Harry. An extremely long cigarette holder. Another
picture: a seven by nine, framed in a creamy embossed
paper, and inscribed "To Vera and the Others—Sargeant."
Sargeant! I did not recognize him. The pictures of him in
the study downstairs were of his early college days and
looked overposed. This one, however, was perhaps flat-
tering; it was an arty picture, with shadows and cigarette
smoke curling up towards his handsome nose and his
deep-set pale eyes. His hair looked darker than Jerome's
and it was cut differently—in a European fashion. He had
outstanding cheekbones, and his smile might have been a
sneer or a snarl had there not been joyful wrinkles around
his eyes. The total effect was positive.

And there were letters. Two packs of letters. I took
them, feeling guilty about it, but not enough so to deter
me, and by the time I got out of the attic and down to my
room I had collected enough rationalizations to push me
through nearly any crime.

They were an assortment of letters, a number being
mundane business letters and a few thank-you letters to
Sargeant from people who had enjoyed his dinner parties,
his cocktail affairs. Many of the letters (most of them, in
fact) seemed needlessly cryptic, e.g., someone who signed
herself Agatha Runcible wrote:

> *Poor darling P is again in a hissy over CD—you
> know, CD is the one we met at the boat party for
> Nora. Well, this will kill you: last week, CD and BG*

left P twiddling her beads at the VVT. Now, really,
how can a sister see Saint Theresa suitably?

It was all as puzzling as the stock exchange, or differential equations. One writer to Sargeant, whose signature was "L. Bloom," wrote less cryptically than the others and wrote literary-type letters that were usually prefaced with a light anecdote about some mutual acquaintance, such as:

. . . but the dear child is too much and not to be
believed. She took her poodle out cruising with her the
other night and walked up and down Third Avenue so
long the poodle fell into extreme exhaustion and had to
be taken home in a taxi. So help me God. You think
that stopped the child? Indeed not. Ten minutes later
Miss Thing was right back in the street, sans *poodle,*
not fatigued a mite.

And then—then one from Roy Flynn. Its frankness was appalling; I found myself running to Della's room in a sweat, and before I knew it I was shouting: "Della! Della!" The closets were empty, except for a cotton belt she'd left behind. There was no aroma of Turkish Kiss Kologne, and the bed was made up tight. *Della! Della!* Why wasn't I nicer to you? There wasn't a sound in the house. No hangers were on the floor and her room was empty. She had gone. She had really gone. I looked down at the crumpled Roy Flynn letter in my hand: sweat faded the ink. The bureau was neat. There was no dust anywhere and in the room there was not Della. Oh, God, why did you have to go, Della?

I don't know how long I stood there in Della's empty room watching the sun go down, lacerating myself with self-pity. It may have been two minutes, it may have been an hour. Then, it was from Della's window I saw—Oh! No! Bertram!

4

Bertram killing Peacock.

I could not believe that the ax in his hand was intended for the neck of the huge bird who followed him to the tree stump near the black grove of trees. I saw him down in the yard there—I thought puttering—putting away lawn equipment, cleaning out the barn. (The lachrymose cow was given away the morning before to a man and his wife who lived northeast of us, near Belle Thompson's.) But when I saw him with the ax, and saw him staring at Peacock for a long time, I ran downstairs and shouted: "What are you going to do?"

His deafness was both a blessing and an inconvenience, depending on his temperament at any given time. Today he would not answer. His eyes studied my face, critically and briefly, and went right back to a contemplative stare in the direction of Peacock's neck. The bird was too stupid to guess; it walked around Bertram as it had always done, and today, in one of its rare displays, it strutted a bit and showed off its stuff. It was pathetically vain. (Aunt Harry had once said the bird was mentally retarded.) Nevertheless, who did

Bertram think he was? God or somebody? It was odd: all I knew was that he came from Poland long ago and I would likely never know much more about him.

He stood there in the soft glare of sundown, in faded overalls, ax in hand, staring at the neck of Peacock. From Bertram's lean face came no hint of the dark plan in his heart, no sign that he was coldly contemplating murder.

"Bertram, you can't! You can't just do that!"

The evening rays sought out the cold blade of the ax playing blue-yellow shadow games upon it, but there was not a hint of apprehension in Peacock's eyes. And he was quick, the executioner, or perhaps Peacock was so benign that Bertram's murderous task was easy. With only a few half-hearted beatings of the wings on the stump at sundown, it was over, but it was at the moment that it was over that the fury without sound came: Peacock, headless, now so blind, and its animation so delayed, scurried and fluttered and staggered in circles, spouting, at the point where its head once had been, dark rust blood in short jerks; it percolated upwards, the blood, and it ran down its feathers and down its breast. The struggle for seeing, for freedom, subsided, and then began again, as though there were one last chance left. In a very final fury the headless bird (and I could *hear* it screaming!) flung itself right and left, as though it were testing ways out of its blind labyrinth, and then, in a sad and ludicrous wobble, it ran into the black grove of trees and fell there, died there, leaving a trail of vermilion drippings on blades of grass.

Bertram held in his hand Peacock's head and his overalls were flecked with red. The ax was dull with the stain from the blood of the fowl.

"Why did you have to do it, Bertram? Damn you, why?" I felt the same terror again—a loss, of something I could not identify—and the blood in my head throbbed in a pain: I felt the ax might well have struck me. "Cold! Ruthless! It's a kind of murder, Bertram!"

With the bloody head still in his hand and soiling the grass, he stood there looking at me under a lock of gray. Then he said, not shouting as I had, but quietly, as though he could hear perfectly: "When a peacock's days are over, they're over."

"What? What? What kind of talk is that? Bertram? 'When a peacock's days are over, they're over.' What kind of talk is that?"

He did not reply. He left the ax on the stump. He walked away. Peacock's head was still in his hand.

5

It stopped raining at ten o'clock and Mrs. Klein wanted to sit by the window and take in the night air. The nurse said it was all right as long as she kept the shawl (one of Aunt Harry's) around her shoulders. This seemed to be a lot of fussiness, for it was hot, too hot to breathe, but I promised I would see that the shawl stayed in place while I sat with her.

She was still uncommunicative, only nodding or shaking her head when it was absolutely necessary. She did not ask for rum and she did not ask for Wordsworth and sometimes she was so still that I thought she was sleeping with her eyes open. Occasionally she would doze, but whenever she woke, in little jerks and blinking of her eyes, she would turn her head from the window to me in apology. It was as though she thought it rude to fall asleep on her company, even though she did not talk. I asked her would she care for me to read to her but she shook her head slightly and smiled only a fraction of an inch. I began reading, silently, and saw, whenever I glanced up, that her head rested on the pillow, and it was turned towards me, watching. She seemed to get some pleasure out of this—just watching. At first it made me very uncomfortable, but as I went along, at the turn of each page, I looked up and smiled; her eyes, those Rachmaninoff eyes, watched me read for quite a time—at least half an hour. I looked again. They were still watching. But they had a peculiar sheen to them—the blue seemed glassy, and the stare penetrated without half trying. I continued to read, but fear struck me and ran my blood cold. I knew her eyes were on me, though I did not look up, and I knew I would have to get up, go over to her. I delayed it, pretended that it would be all right, even as the chill grew in me, and playfully I lifted my head and smiled. I need not have. I could no longer pretend that I did not know life had gone out of those pale blue eyes, while staring upon me. She died somewhere between ten o'clock and ten forty-five, sitting in her chair, watching me read.

It was such a short time ago that she had stood, on another afternoon, in a veil, over the plot next to Aunt Harry's. Now she was being lowered there, under a rainy sky. Mark and Marcus, dressed to the nines, came from the East to her funeral, and there were a few other faces, but they were faces I did not know. Bertram stood apart from the crowd, in private mourning, with a black suit that shone with age, and with a black hat in his hands. Belle Thompson was there, too—probably to have a catharsis, though she was careful to stand far away from Patricia Jo.

There were flowers, there were flowers. And a titmouse flew about the cemetery.

As we left the grave I passed Belle, who stood behind a tree, looking deep into a compact to fix her lips. She said, without moving her eyes from the mirror, "Hi, honey-bunch. Still sore at me?"

I said, "Hello."

"Before you go off to that school of yours, you oughta run up and read me one of them sonnets." She said it without provocation, without teasing, as though she'd passed the time of day, and not even once did she look up from her mirror.

Patricia Jo came up along with Jerome in time to see Belle thumping her heels through the high grass, swinging her purse. "What's that awful woman doing here?" Patricia Jo asked, her eyes following Belle's peregrinations around tombstones.

"Come," Jerome said, as though he were in no mood to squabble.

The huge black limousine (not Jerome's) was large enough for six, so I rode with them—Patricia Jo and Jerome, and their sons. We all looked, including the chauffeur, towards the graves of Mrs. Klein and Aunt Harry, and we would have driven off had we all not noticed an odd thing, a strange thing: at the deserted graves we saw Bertram. He was kneeling in the fresh sand where Mrs. Klein had been buried. His knees were deep in the sand and his head was bent slightly towards the flowers. His grief, at some distance away, was heard in its terrible silence. Except for a gray lock of hair that blew to his face, and the capering titmouse above his head, there was no movement, no indication of life. We in the limousine could not take our eyes from him, and we were, I'm sure, in accord: his grief was deeper than ours, more painful and immense. It was as if a stranger—and Bertram was a stranger, in a way—were staking a claim, or perhaps it was more of an awareness that *we* were strangers watching someone else's great misfortune, as though we were eavesdropping on someone's most private moment. It was as plain as day: Bertram had loved Mrs. Klein, and this realization came, I felt, simultaneously to all of us who sat in the car, including the twins, including the chauffeur. How long had he loved her? Had she loved him? Was it an unrequited affair, or had it been vibrant and clandestine, and had it been in process for years? We, the strangers, would never ask, nor do I think we would ever speak of it, for we had seen a grief too naked, and for that love—now broken by death—we did not know whether to be proud or sad.

It was the chauffeur who performed the discreet act: he started the motor and drove away without instructions to do so, as though he were at that moment the pilot and controller of our lives. All heads turned from the graveyard, slowly and at once, and no one spoke the entire trip back to Green Acorns.

Two days later, in early evening before the crickets began, I left for Ithaca. Jerome sat in the back seat with me and talked all the way to the airport, consoling me, cheering me, telling me I had nothing to worry about. He probably thought his dispensations of cheer were successful, for as I boarded the plane and said good-by, I smiled. But the smile was not really for Jerome, even if it should have been. I smiled because I heard, in the midst of the dissonant

McNally Editions reissues books that are not widely known but have stood the test of time, that remain as singular and engaging as when they were written. Available in the US wherever books are sold or by subscription from mcnallyeditions.com.

1. Han Suyin, *Winter Love*
2. Penelope Mortimer, *Daddy's Gone A-Hunting*
3. David Foster Wallace, *Something to Do with Paying Attention*
4. Kay Dick, *They*
5. Margaret Kennedy, *Troy Chimneys*
6. Roy Heath, *The Murderer*
7. Manuel Puig, *Betrayed by Rita Hayworth*
8. Maxine Clair, *Rattlebone*
9. Akhil Sharma, *An Obedient Father*
10. Gavin Lambert, *The Goodby People*
11. Wyatt Harlan, *Elbowing the Seducer*
12. Lion Feuchtwanger, *The Oppermanns*
13. Gary Indiana, *Rent Boy*
14. Alston Anderson, *Lover Man*
15. Michael Clune, *White Out*
16. Martha Dickinson Bianchi, *Emily Dickinson Face to Face*
17. Ursula Parrott, *Ex-Wife*
18. Margaret Kennedy, *The Feast*
19. Henry Bean, *The Nenoquich*
20. Mary Gaitskill, *The Devil's Treasure*
21. Elizabeth Mavor, *A Green Equinox*
22. Dinah Brooke, *Lord Jim at Home*
23. Phyllis Paul, *Twice Lost*
24. John Bowen, *The Girls*
25. Henry Van Dyke, *Ladies of the Rachmaninoff Eyes*
26. Duff Cooper, *Operation Heartbreak*
27. Jane Ellen Harrison, *Reminiscences of a Student's Life*
28. Robert Shaplen, *Free Love*